BINSTEAD'S SAFARI

Also by Rachel Ingalls

THEFT
THE MAN WHO WAS LEFT BEHIND
MRS. CALIBAN
I SEE A LONG JOURNEY
THE PEARLKILLERS
THE END OF TRAGEDY
FOUR STORIES
DAYS LIKE TODAY
TIMES LIKE THESE
BLACK DIAMOND
THREE MASQUERADES

Rachel Ingalls

Binstead's Safari

a novel

A NEW DIRECTIONS PAPERBOOK

Manufactured in the United States of America
New Directions Books are printed on acid-free paper
First published in the UK by Faber and Faber Limited
and in the United States by Simon and Schuster
First published as New Directions Paperbook 1433 in 2019
Design by Erik Rieselbach

Library of Congress Cataloging-in-Publication Data
Names: Ingalls, Rachel, author.
Title: Binstead's safari : a novel / Rachel Ingalls.
Description: First New Directions paperback edition. |
New York : New Directions Publishing Corporation, 2019. |
"A New Directions paperbook."
Identifiers: LCCN 2018039756 (print) | LCCN 2018041148 (ebook) |
ISBN 9780811228473 (ebook) | ISBN 9780811228466 (alk. paper)
Classification: LCC PS3559.N38 (ebook) |
LCC PS3559.N38 B56 2019 (print) | DDC 813/.54–dc23
LC record available at https://lccn.loc.gov/2018039756

2 4 6 8 10 9 7 5 3 1

New Directions Books are published for James Laughlin
by New Directions Publishing Corporation
80 Eighth Avenue, New York 10011

BINSTEAD'S SAFARI

STAN BINSTEAD AND his wife, Millie, reached London early in the morning. They both felt heavy and tired from their flight and were already weighed down by an emotion that made for even greater lassitude – a kind of inertia, intermittently broken by irritable indecisiveness. In the army they call it combat fatigue.

He hadn't wanted to bring her along; she kept pleading until he gave in. No sentimental argument would have persuaded him, but she wasn't in the habit of thinking up such maneuvers. She would never ask, "How could you leave me?" or tell him, "You don't love me." She had just said, "But I've never seen London. I've never been to Africa. It's the only chance I'll ever have to go on a really nice vacation. I've never been out of the country at all." It was true. She hadn't even been away from New England before the first time he'd taken her to visit his family.

"The money it would cost," he had said, as if otherwise, naturally, it would be all right. He needed to go, for research. That was what he said. Her presence would be a luxury.

Then, right on time, as though planned that way, her Great Aunt Edna died, leaving her a nice little sum of money and several glass cases filled with knick-knacks that would have been useless all the time they were going into the collection, yet were now in fashion and could be sold for quite a lot. Millie had been fond of the old lady and was overjoyed about the bequest. How nice of her it had been, she kept saying. How thoughtful.

They dozed for part of the morning in the twin beds of their hotel room, had lunch downstairs and made plans for their stay. Stan hadn't been able to get hold of his friend, Jack, who – according to the girl who answered the phone when he called up – was still away on a long weekend in the country. It was some kind of holiday in town; all the stores were closed. Millie wanted to take one of the tourist bus rides with him. He told her no, she should go herself and he would stay in the room and read the papers.

"Oh, Stan," she said. "You come three thousand miles just to read the newspapers? You can buy the same ones at home."

"Well, I don't want to go on one of those tours."

"Okay, we'll walk."

"It's raining."

Millie's face took on a peculiar look, as though parts of it had shrunk. "We'll walk in the rain," she said.

That was what they ended up doing. They went through a few parks, saw some fine crescents and cornices and squares, and Millie asked him at least three times if he wasn't glad she'd remembered to pack the umbrellas. As they walked forward through the drizzle, he thought: *It's all right sometimes, then suddenly it's like this. I was foolish. I should just have left. I should have said: Take a vacation wherever you want to, as long as it's a long way away from me.*

They got lost, found an Italian restaurant that was open, and had supper. They drank twice as much as usual, becoming mildly drunk, and were out on the wet streets again, feeling befuddled but more enthusiastic about London than they had been before.

Stan said, "This is a great town."

"My feet are turning all funny," Millie told him, in a high little voice like a child at a birthday party.

"Come on, funnyfoot," he said close to her ear.

He put his arm around her. She had an idea that at last things were going to be all right. Back at the hotel, they made love for the first time in many months. But, in the morning, nothing had changed. They had breakfast, he spent half an hour telephoning, and was finally able to find his friend, Jack.

"Will you be all right shopping, and so on?" he asked her.

"Can't I meet Jack?"

"I think it would be sort of boring for you."

"But I'd like to come."

"We're just going to be talking shop the whole time. And catching up on all the years we haven't seen each other."

She smiled, and thought: *So, it's you who would be bored if I came along.*

"The whole day?"

"Well, look. There are all those tours you wanted to go on, and the museums, and if you could try to get some of the tickets, that would be a help. Unless – no, I won't know till I talk to Jack. I want to see some of the footage from that documentary he worked on. They may set it up for the evening. You go enjoy yourself, see the town. I'll do the American Express and the Africa part."

"You don't want to do anything together?"

"I've got these meetings. I told you. And I've got to do some research in the libraries. Listen," he said, nervousness coming into his face and voice, "I told you before we got here, long before: I'm supposed to be working. You wanted to come along – fine, but I can't hold your hand."

"I only asked."

He went to a meeting and had lunch with some of his colleagues.

*

The trip would never become a second honeymoon, as she had begun to hope the night before. No chance of that. It would be another eight or ten months before he decided he wanted her again.

She went to a museum. She liked museums, but it always took as much time to read the information as to look at the things.

This bowl is decorated by a process known as cloisonné. *This figure represents the goddess Hathor. The dwarf in the corner is probably the royal sandalbearer.*

There were crowds everywhere. She got on a bus to go back, but it went in the wrong direction. After doing the same kind of thing several times, she walked or took taxis from the Underground stations. The Underground was the one part of the city she understood immediately. It was exactly the way it promised to be. When the chart said west, that was what it meant, straight as an arrow. The plans on the walls coincided with real maps of the city and the electric lines were just as they ought to be: left, right, up, down. And each one was in a different color.

She went to all the big museums, one after another, visited a couple of the parks farther out of town, walked through the botanical gardens and went to a matinée. She bought two pairs of shoes, and began to enjoy herself.

Stan was off meeting people with his friend. And who knew who else. That first evening he'd gone out alone, he had come back drunk. And the next, he'd tottered in so late that when she turned on the light, he said he was too tired to talk and if she made a fuss or even said a word, he'd never speak to her again. On the next day, the rain stopped for an entire twenty-four-hour stretch and she had tea alone in an upstairs tea-room filled with little chairs and tables that seemed made for children. She saw exactly the right present for her mother-in-law, attended an afternoon piano concert, was caught in the rain afterwards, couldn't find her way back for an hour, and got her period.

They went to the theater together once. She asked why this friend, Jack, couldn't join them. Conferences, Stan said.

*

She was going from shop to shop one day, looking for a nice purse to send her sister, Betty. The sun was out, she waited at the curb for the traffic lights to change, and then when they did, caught sight of herself in the plate glass of a store opposite. She saw an ordinary woman, mooning along the street, who looked like somebody else. She thought: *My God, I look like somebody's mother.* The thought paralyzed her for an instant. She let the lights change a second time before she moved with the crowd. She crossed the street towards her reflection, stopped outside the building and pretended that she was waiting for someone. She wanted to be still and think for a while, but there was no place to sit down.

If I don't do something, she thought, *nobody else will. I've got to do something. It's already too late anyway, so why not? Could anything be worse than the way things are?*

She went and had her hair cut, bought some clothes and earrings, makeup, bead necklaces, a bracelet and some nail polish which she never used but suddenly thought she might try. She decided to go out alone in the evening. Stan would be back late that night too. He had warned her that every night was going to be like this.

She stood outside the opera house and bought a ticket at the side entrance near the back, where people were selling because their favorite dancer had been replaced by someone else. She had thought it would be an opera, but it was a ballet: the girl in a pink costume, men giving her roses, the wicked witch putting a spell on her and the prince eventually finding her and waking her up. True love, rescue, marriage. Happily ever after.

At the end, when the girl next to her screamed, "Bravo," Millie yelled too. She was carried away. Everyone around her was shouting appreciation. She was no longer sure that she wanted to go on to Africa. She liked London. And afterwards, near midnight as she leaned towards her image in the hotel mirror, she thought she appeared completely different. She looked better.

Stan still hadn't come in. She heard him much later and put her arm across her eyes until he banged into the wall and hit the switches that turned off the bedside lamp and lit up the one near the bathroom.

The first thing he said to her in the morning was, "What have you done to yourself?"

"For heaven's sake," she told him. "I had a haircut, that's

all." He looked astonished. She never answered back like that. But he hadn't noticed the other changes in her.

*

He was busy with his own adventures; free, on vacation and being paid for it. No more students and their theses, or committee work, classes and exams. No one else's theories but his own. It felt great. Not even Millie could spoil it.

He walked out of the British Museum, down the steps, over to the gates, and saw straight ahead of him across the street a black-painted doorway and, in white capital letters on the glass above it, the single word: MAGIC. He wasn't sure how the numbers went, so he crossed over to the pub on the corner and checked the sequence as he strolled by: the Museum Tavern, the knitwear shop advertising "kilts, shetlands, cashmeres, gifts," a door marked "50," then the Magic shop, which had a sign hanging outside that showed a white rabbit being pulled out of a black hat. Down the hat ran yellow words: *Davenport's tricks, jokes, puzzles.* A block of flats nearby bore a small plaque indicating that it was the Helen Graham House, YWCA. And a couple of doors beyond that, he found the right number.

He climbed all the way to the top floor because the elevator was full of people moving laundry baskets.

Jack said, "Stan. Christ, I don't believe it. Come on in."

The living room windows looked across to the pediment above the main entrance of the museum. The view was good, although slightly to the side, and gave the building the appearance of being in motion, like an immense gray aircraft carrier passing by above the trees. But the sightlines still took in the whole sweep. It was possible to make out the carvings: the turtle on the right, the crocodile at the left, mythological people in between.

Jack said, "It's the Y who've got the really good view, I guess, but this is okay too. Girlfriend of mine told me she never noticed all those allegorical characters up there before, and over in a corner somebody's doing something very unusual to a dog."

"I can't see it. Probably looking through a microscope at it. The whole business is supposed to be about social progress, isn't it?"

"Ah, those old-time optimists. Such faith in the rational outcome. You're looking pretty good for somebody stuck in the academic rut. What do you do – swim, box?"

"Squash." Tuesday, Thursday, Saturday, every week. Monday and Wednesday were free, Friday was Myra. Sunday at home, or maybe out for a walk.

"A drink?" Jack suggested. "I hope you aren't actually in training, or anything. We can go around the corner for lunch, back here, and – listen, come along tonight. I'll get Shirley to bring a friend."

Stan hesitated, then said, "All right."

"All right drink, or all right tonight?"

"Both."

"Way to go, Stanley."

During the afternoon they worked their way through a good deal of liquor and caught up on most of the news as well as talking about old times. They had been college roommates. As the sky grew darker, Stan confessed that his marriage was not happy. He couldn't even remember any more whether it had ever been happy, but he never used to tell anyone. Now that it was probably too late for anything to save it, he could say what it was like. Jack nodded; he had been divorced for seven years. His ex-wife was back in the States with the two children, a second husband, and a third and fourth child. The new husband had had two of his own by a first marriage, too. "So it's quite a circus," Jack said. "They sent me a composite Christmas card this year with a photograph on it. Incredible. Looked like a crowd scene from *The Ten Commandments*."

Stan talked about the Africa trip. His subject was folklore. A colleague in Switzerland, a Dr. Adler, had brought back a story about an East African lion cult, which raised some interesting questions on the nature of kingship and the practice and development of cult worship. Adler had taped chants and ceremonies from three different regions, and when he was in America before the spring term, had given Stan copies and translations.

"He's been sick lately. And he gave me permission to follow it up."

Jack lolled back in his chair and smiled. He said, "Oh, Stanley. Don't you know when the local yokels are pulling your leg?"

Stan shrugged. He sank farther down in the sofa cushions. "Adler's a good researcher," he said. "Very sound."

"Look, I just came back from all those places a few months ago."

"I know, I know. That's why –"

"Wait a second. I may not know all of Africa, but I do know what this thing is: it's like the Leopard Men. You know about them? You do something wrong and the Leopard Men will get you: eerie music, growls in the night, body found at dawn – *The Hound of the Baskervilles* isn't in it. But that's all hooey. What's really going on is just an old-fashioned protection racket. You give these guys their money or they come around some night dressed up in leopard skins and wearing these special gloves with metal claws on them, and then they rip you to pieces with the things and say the leopards got you. Sometimes it's genuine. It probably started out that way."

"You mean, there was a genuine cult, a religious order that worshiped the leopards?"

"No, no. Forget all that. When I say genuine, I only mean that in the beginning what happened was: the village elders try to keep everyone in line, but if there are a couple of people or families who start acting up, they issue a warning to them and if nobody pays any attention to it, they give the high-sign to their friendly neighborhood hit-man in the spotted cloak. I think sometimes they used to be connected with the medicine man, didn't they?"

"Maybe it wouldn't make any difference."

"Come on. Either you've got a cult, or you've got Africa's answer to Capone."

"But if these stories and songs and rituals have sprung up, then they're genuine even if the thing they're based on isn't."

"Sounds crazy."

"Not to me. It's the way a religious movement starts."

"Like I said. Crazy."

"The mechanics of delusion. In action," Stan said.

Outside it was dark early, wet and chilly, although certainly not cold compared to home. He remembered to call Millie. That was another delusion: hers. She had so many. She had them instead of thoughts. He was beginning to get drunk, though he didn't hear it in his voice and it was all right over the phone. Sometimes he pitied her, but mostly he just felt desperation. She irritated the hell out of him, too.

Jack called his two girlfriends, Shirley and Kathy. He stretched and yawned after putting the receiver down. "We can have a foursome," he said. "Oh-ho. If you could see your face, Stanley. What did you think I meant?"

They took the girls out to eat. Shirley was dark, quick and impertinent, Kathy a blonde who giggled all the time. Both of them worked as secretaries at the BBC, where Jack had met them, and both were pretty.

They went to a noisy discotheque and left after fifteen minutes, sampled three different pubs, and then took a taxi back to the flat. The girls headed for the bathroom. Kathy kicked off her shoes on the way. They were all more or less drunk. Stan flopped down on the sofa.

Jack asked, "How do you feel, Stanley?"

"Wonderful. How you doing yourself, Livingstone?"

"Oh, I'm feeling no pain. Might as well make a night of it, hm?" He went to the desk, took a small box out of one of the drawers, and brought it over.

"Ever tried any of this stuff?"

"Genuine mind-bending material?"

"The real thing."

"Are you kidding?"

"So?" Jack said. "What are you scared of? Afraid you'll like it?"

Stan looked at the box and looked up at Jack. He wasn't all that drunk and he saw what was coming next. He said, "When you told me we could have a foursome, that was exactly what you did mean, wasn't it?"

"Sure. Why not? Don't tell me those stories about wife-swapping parties in New England colleges are just propaganda from the tourist trade."

They had nearly three weeks in London. Millie kept walking through museums, went to movies, wrote postcards and thought about sending packages home to his parents and sister. At the right time – convenient for them and not for her – she phoned her own parents, and then his. And she tried to get Stan to help with some shopping, but he left it to her to choose presents. No one at home expected a thing, he said. Why waste the short time they had?

*

She wanted another dress, too – maybe he could help her pick one. But, he wouldn't. That was her business. He thought it was a little strange, anyway. She had never bought herself unnecessary and fancy clothes.

"You've been spending money like water," he told her. "Where are you going to wear all those things? We're going into the African bush, not to a cocktail party."

"I bet they have cocktails in Africa, too."

"Not the part we're going to."

She took a tour out to Hampton Court and on the same day visited the zoo. The place was almost deserted; she strolled past owls, monkeys, seals, parrots, bears. A family of three took photographs of each other in the distance and two girls walked by, one of them wheeling a baby in a push-chair.

She went to look at the tigers, where she stood not far from a boy of twelve or so, who was listening to some kind of taped commentary on the animals. There were no tigers in Africa, she knew that; only in India and farther east. The boy was fiddling with the earpiece and the volume. Millie overheard the voice from the tape saying, "Note the white spot behind the ears." She looked. The nearest tiger rolled smoothly by and moved away. Sure enough, at the back of each ear was a large, round, white spot. It interested and amazed her: that every tiger should have white circles on its ears. Why were the markings there – so the cubs could follow the parents through the twilit jungle without losing them? It was a mystery.

She couldn't find the right way out, and, in trying to get back to where she'd been, came across the pandas. They sat eating their bamboo shoots with delicate bites and didn't hurry their meal. She thought they were charming. And they were very civilized eaters. Maybe that was the trouble. They certainly had their problems. Their failed love-life had been on the front pages of all the daily papers. *Never mind,* she thought. *There are lots of us.*

On the day before they left, she discovered the one museum on her list that she'd missed. She just had time to fit it in.

A guard looked at her bag as she entered, and asked her to leave her umbrella in the cloakroom. She picked up a leaflet from a table near the stairs and glanced at the diagram of the rooms.

There were several exhibitions on at the same time: Mexican turquoise inlaid figurines, Captain Cook's voyages, African masks, and all the regular exhibits and displays. She wandered around from floor to floor, leaning over glass cases, scanning explanatory printed cards. *Cloth with border of stylized eye emblem* she read, and looked closely at a small, dark rectangle inside a large, white one: the iris inside the cornea, she supposed. *Axe handle carved with picture of Indian slaying enemy* read another card. The enemy warrior was tiny, the Indian extremely large. What it means to be the winner. And if you lose, you die. That hadn't changed.

She looked at two red and yellow Hawaiian cloaks made out of parrot feathers, studied a canoe and a swordfish of black wood and mother-of-pearl, and reached the section full of objects from aboriginal life: bones, snail-like decorations which were maps, apparently; either of the world or the heavens. Not far from the collection of boomerangs lay a dark wooden object that looked like a thole pin. Its descriptive tag said: *Implement for making toeholds in trees.*

"It's a wonderful town for anybody who lives alone," she said to Stan later in the day. "You could never get bored. You could never get lonely."

He waited for her to bring out all the little pieces of entertainment she had saved up to tell him, but she left it there. She no longer had the eager, pathetic look, hoping to please; nor the stunned, expressionless stare. London had changed her. He was glad. If only she could make some kind of attachment outside, things might be better. He might even be able to leave her – who could tell?

She went over the list of presents she'd send off in the mail the next morning, their last. Better leave a lot of time, pack that night. They might celebrate a little.

"Shall we go out someplace special on our last night?"

"I sort of promised Jack."

"And I'm still never going to meet him?"

"We're just always talking about –"

"All right, I know. I'll see if I can get a ticket to go to another ballet."

It was because he was ashamed of her, of course. He didn't want his friend Jack to see the miserable frump he'd ended up with. Even though she looked fine now, with her new clothes and her haircut. Of course it might be another woman again

– that was possible, too. Jack might just be the excuse he gave. Or Jack might not exist.

She bought a ticket at the opera house that evening from a girl with glasses and long, straight yellow hair, who said, "Dowell's off, you know. It's Wall tonight."

Millie said, "Oh?"

"Is that all right?"

"Isn't this one any good?"

"Oh yes, of course. He's very good, only he's not the one I wanted to see tonight. I'm seeing him next week."

"I understand. You have your favorite."

"Yes. She's lovely, of course."

Millie climbed the stairs, bought a program and sat in her seat. She was early. She read through the notes about the plot: about Romeo and Juliet, whom she already knew about, and the composer, whom she'd never heard of and couldn't pronounce, and all the dancers and the choreographer, who was a modern one. She thought about Stan and the rest of the trip. When they'd been back home she would have taken any chance to get away, and as far as possible. But now she felt safe in London and didn't want to leave. The thought of flying off again made her worry. He was probably right: here, she could go out and do things, but where would she go in Africa? If they were way out in the middle of nowhere, she wouldn't be able to do anything but sit in the tent.

During the balcony scene, she cried a little. She was also very moved by the argument between Juliet and her parents. *That's the way I should have been,* she thought. *I should have talked back and said what I wanted myself.*

In the first interval, she had a cup of coffee and unobtrusively examined the people around her, some of whom looked like dancers. It was fine being alone. Several other people were on their own. It was better than being with Stan. He wouldn't have liked it. He had even said: what a hell of a thing to do to a good play.

*

He was saying goodbye. They were in the living room. Jack was laughing at him.

"You take it lightly," Stan said.

"Sure. No use getting morbid about things."

"You think all emotion is morbid."

"Look, four guys I worked with went out like a light last year. Just like that. Ashes to ashes, Stan. Now you see them, now you don't. Abracadabra. One of them stepped on a mine, one of them caught a ricochet, one of them was in that plane in the Canary Islands, one of them was grabbed out of his taxi by some secret service heavies who said later it must have been political fanatics. So, what I think is: I hope they had all the good times they could squeeze in before they got it. I hope they never said no to something they wanted, just to be polite or because somebody didn't think it would be ladylike. The purpose of this, all this, is pleasure. If you don't even like it – hell, it's wasted on you. Get out and let somebody else enjoy it. I mean it, Stanley."

Shirley walked into the room. She said, "What is this Stanley and Livingstone thing?"

"It started the first time we met. Because he kept calling me Stanley."

"Isn't that your name?"

"No, my middle name's Dunstan, that's all."

"What's your first name?"

"Don't tell her," Stan said, "or I'll tell yours."

"My first name is John."

"That's what he tells everybody."

"Come on. He's kidding."

Kathy called from the next room, "What are you up to now?"

"All these years we've been calling each other Stanley and Livingstone," Jack said, "and now suddenly you're going off to Africa and I just got back from there."

They drank one another's health, and, before the party broke up, Jack added a warning. He told Stan, "If it looks like I'm right about the protection racket side of it, steer clear. Those things can be just as prickly in an African mudhole as back in Little Italy, believe me."

Millie leaned up against the window and looked down as they flew over. She said, "It's so different. It doesn't look at all like the way I imagined Africa."

Stan said, "What did you expect – grass huts?"

She didn't answer. He thought: *Of course, that's exactly what she did expect.*

Their room was ready for them. All the arrangements, from airport to hotel, went smoothly. Stan felt slightly out of step because of the sudden change in temperature, altitude, and the general look of things – the tremendous variation and mixture of peoples and languages. He realized some hours later, when he had a moment to think about it, that for once Millie wasn't tied up in knots by a nervous reaction to the strangeness of her surroundings. She was actually smiling and looking around with interest.

They rested for a couple of hours at the hotel, together but separate, as usual. Millie unpacked a few clothes and hung them up. Later in the day, they went to the offices of the safari company. They met Ian Foster, a man in his early sixties, who was to be their professional hunter; he was short, husky, very tanned and had a close-cut brindled beard he later told them had started as a way of protecting himself against a sun eczema. He looked weather-beaten and trustworthy. A muscular young man, blond and blue-eyed, joined them and was introduced as Nicholas Fairchild; he might have been in his late twenties or early thirties but seemed younger, like a college athlete. Ian referred to him as his partner.

They talked about clothes, firearms, licenses and recording equipment. Ian walked over to a map on the wall and drew his right hand across it. Stan thought about the projected route for a moment, then tapped his finger over three different places.

Millie studied the photographs on the walls and gazed at the one large animal head in the room, up above the lintel: a buffalo, with the horns that began on the middle of its forehead like an old-fashioned haircut parted in the center or a low-fitting matador's hat. Nicholas followed her eyes. "They're the worst," he said.

"I can imagine. It looks huge."

"That's not important. It's the fact that the boss makes him almost invulnerable, and they won't give in. Most beasts will let one alone. Buff goes out of his way to hunt you down. Nasty."

She made a face, commiserating.

"Are you shooting?" he asked.

"Not me. I'm just coming along for the ride. Trying not to get in anybody's way."

"Jolly good."

Even in London, Millie hadn't met anyone who said, "Jolly good." She was delighted.

They looked through stores, went wandering around the streets and were measured for their clothes. This time, Stan didn't seem to mind the shopping. They also tried out different kinds of rifles and shotguns.

"Not for my wife," he said.

"No?" Ian looked disappointed. "You're not going to shoot at all?"

Millie said, "I don't know how."

"We'll soon teach you. All part of the service."

"Fine. Then I'll take whatever gun fits."

Ian laughed.

"You aren't serious?" Stan asked.

She said, "Well, I think it's always nice to be on the safe side, like knowing how to drive a car, or swim. You never know when you may need to. As far as the shooting goes, I wouldn't want to kill anything I wasn't going to eat, and actually I'm so squeamish I'd rather let somebody else do it, but I really would just like to know how."

"Target practice isn't any good," Stan told her. "If you're ever going to shoot anything, it's going to be moving."

"I'll leave it all up to Mr. Foster," she said, turning to him. "You're the expert."

"Right you are. We'll start tomorrow. Come out to the farm for lunch and we'll see what we can do."

*

There was some hitch in the preparations for the safari, but it was the fault of other people. The original plan had been to organize a large, double safari; Ian would take charge of the Binsteads and Nicholas would be working with a couple named Whiteacre, who were monstrously rich and intended to do a lot of serious hunting while traveling slowly or stationed in one place for many weeks at a time. The Whiteacres were going to be accompanied by great amounts of luxury equipment and their main site could serve as a base camp for other hunters, especially for someone like Stan, who wanted to visit distant villages lying among parts of the country poor in game. Now the Whiteacres were cabling that they thought they might postpone the date, or maybe not, or perhaps a friend or two might be coming with them. Ian wanted to give them a couple of days and then divide the safari in two. Everyone could join up later and there would be no difference in the money. Stan's position would be the same; with the university's help, he was now semiofficial. The costs were taken care of. He paid the extras, of course, but he was hoping to get a book out of the expedition, and that would even up his expenses afterwards.

The gist of the book was already down on paper. It was a theory about mythic character and its relation to the society that gives rise to it. He was especially interested in the changes the central personality underwent as different generations of storytellers shaped the incidents in their hero's career.

*

Ian showed them around the city. They went into shops, to bars, including the hotel bar, had restaurants pointed out, met people walking down the street. Everyone knew Ian. And all at once, everyone knew the Binsteads, too. It was like being in a small town, except for the fact that there were high modern buildings and the crowds were of many nationalities and races and were dressed in all manner of clothing. During a walk of only four blocks Millie saw two women wearing silk saris, an African tribesman in a ceremonial dress decorated with green fur and black feathers, and a white man, dark as a gypsy, who looked as if he had come straight off the plains and was carrying a snake around his left arm. Ian nodded to them all.

In the evening, they sat outside on the hotel terrace. Ian was their guest, but the talk was of the trip rather than general chat.

"Anything you can tell me about the whole area," Stan said.

"That's a tall order."

"Especially any stories about lions."

"You mean travelers' tales? The one that got away?"

"I mean lion worship."

"Well, there's the Masai and the spearhunts, but is that what you had in mind? Initiation trials – that sort of thing?"

"No, not at all." Stan began to talk about the Swiss researches and theories. In the middle of the explanations it was settled that they all call each other by their first names, which would have been unheard of only ten years before, but now it would be silly not to.

"What Dr. Adler told me, and what he's given to me in translation, is a series of linked stories about a man with supernatural powers in battle and medicine, and love. When he's in a tough situation, he can turn himself into a lion, because his bravery was so great that the lions gave him the ability: to make himself one of them."

"That's a new one on me," Ian said.

Millie, who had been left out of the talk, suddenly exclaimed, "Like Superman."

"No, Millie. Not like Superman."

Ian laughed. "I'll get you out there and interpret for you," he said. "The rest is up to you." He said goodnight and left early, before the dancing began.

Millie and Stan watched for a while, without joining in. As the hotel guests and their friends became drunker, the overall air of comradeship increased. Names were exchanged, people danced with each other's wives and husbands. It was the kind of thing that happened on board ship. Most of the couples wouldn't know each other in two days' time. Talk grew louder, the music slowed down, and Stan began to yawn. The black waiters and bar attendants looked on silently, doing their work quickly and politely, as they had before Independence.

In the morning, Stan checked with the government officials he had spoken to over the phone. He spent an hour with three of them who were helpful, interested, and glad to be able to act together in such a simple matter – in other words, something that wasn't political. At least, that was the way it seemed. There was a strange reserve between the men, as though they might have been quarreling or talking about some unpleasant subject just before he'd come into the room. He was handed a load of papers, all stamped and signed, and went on to talk to a Frenchman named Lavalle about anthropology. Stan told him what Jack had said about the probabilities of fraud.

"Yes, quite possibly," Lavalle said. "One must be there, where it is taking place. That's the only way to find out. It can go the other way too, you know." He told a brief tale about a Canadian scholar who, against all advice from the professional hunters, mounted an expedition to a part of the country that couldn't conceivably be interesting, camped there for many weeks until the rainy season, and returned with a thick typescript describing ceremonies and rituals no one had known of before.

"All fantasy," Lavalle added.

And the Canadian had been crazy enough to think he could get away with it. He had submitted the work to his university press for publication. Fortunately, some of his colleagues had looked through the document and saved him. For a while, no one knew whether or not he was going to be fired. Then they found out that he had made a few alterations to the book and sold it for a stupendous sum to an independent film producer.

"The last we heard of him, he had retired from his university duties and was negotiating for the foreign-language paperback sales."

Stan liked the story, but said that that was a scholarly fraud. What he was afraid of was what Jack had called a genuine fraud.

"As I say, you must see for yourself. Go there. Look at everything. And be careful. Who have you with your team?"

"Ian Foster."

"In that case, there will be no problem. Ian is one of the best. Nicholas too, but the older generation has known Ian longer. That's important, especially here. We've had enormous changes in the past forty years. Upheavals, one could say. It makes a bond."

*

Millie had taken one of the hotel tours through the game park. Stan saw her as she got out of the bus; she looked young and elegant next to several fat women and seemed to be on terms of the greatest friendship with everyone there, calling people by their names as she said goodbye. But when he asked her, "How was it?" she just said, "It was very nice. How was your morning?" He told her his morning had been fine. Naturally, he realized, her answer was simply the kind he himself usually gave.

"Well," he asked, "what did you see?"

"Oh, everything."

"Such as what, Millie?"

"Animals."

"Rabbits, cows?"

"Elephants. Antelopes. Zebras. Rhinoceroses," she said. "Lions."

"Rhinoceros."

"Rhinos. Nothing close-up. And giraffes."

"Which did you like best?" he said, and thought: *What am I doing? This is like playtime with the three-year-olds. I'd like to hit her.*

"I don't have favorites," she told him. "I liked them all. That's what was nice – there were so many. All different, all interesting, living together. Mohammed said they're going to ban big game hunting soon."

Mohammed must have been the driver. Stan said, "They'd lose a lot of income if they did. It might be a disaster."

"They could get the same amount by just running photographic safaris and building a few more hotels where you can look out of your room and see the herds of wild animals grazing right there on the terrace. Don't you think so?"

"I don't know. Maybe. It would be a blow to Ian and Nicholas."

"They'd just join the Department of Environment and Conservation. They'd be hired to cull the herds."

"Cull the herds? Where do you get all this high-flown technical jargon?"

"I got some books out of the library before we left home."

"Well, I wouldn't believe everything you read in travel books."

"Why not? They were all written by the people who live out here. At least, I think they were."

A battered landrover came to pick them up and take them out to the Fosters' house. They were carried at a smart lick, though not at the breakneck speed they had feared at first sight of the machine. The driver's name was Abdullah. He'd stuck a quotation from the Koran on the windshield and reinforced it with an evil-eye charm that hung from the mirror. Everyone in Africa, Stan thought, seemed to have a religion and to proclaim it without self-consciousness. Even the Europeans and their descendants probably went to church a lot. He was sure they did; it was that kind of place. And why, then, shouldn't there be a resurgence of animal-spirit cults? It would tie in with the new nation's desire to reestablish its cultural and racial heritage as it had been before other people had entered the country bringing different economies, tools, machines, different weapons and clothes, different gods.

"You come from United States of America?" Abdullah asked.

Stan said yes, Millie at the same time said, "London," and then corrected herself, adding, "just the past couple of weeks."

"I was in Europe once," Abdullah said. He pronounced the word so that it had three syllables. "Spain," he added.

"What did you think of it?" Stan asked.

"I hate it," Abdullah answered in a loud whisper. "I hate it, I hate it, I hate it, I hate it."

In the back seat, where Abdullah had insisted on putting

them, Millie and Stan looked at each other sideways. Abdullah continued to express his hatred. The inflection of his voice didn't falter. As soon as he showed signs of letting up, Millie asked, "Why did you hate it?" Stan pinched her arm hard, but too late.

Abdullah began: the devils, the pigs, the dogs who put him in a filthy room like a box, they say you undesirable alien, you are bad to come here, you don't have food what you want, you take what you get and you pay for the boat or you go to jail, may they die in unspeakable agonies.

At the end of the drive, when they had climbed from the car and were walking towards the bungalow out of earshot, Stan said, "What the hell got into you? Couldn't you see he was just itching for you to give him his cue?"

"Don't be silly, Stan. Would you have missed all that for anything? If half the things he said are true –"

"They aren't."

"How do you know? You've never been a penniless stow-away caught by the Immigration Department."

Ian came out on the porch to meet them and bring them inside.

The house was neat and comfortable. There was a lot of light wood everywhere, carved statues, masks, mounted trophies, paintings, bright rugs on the floor and chintz covers patterned and flowering on chairs and couches. Pippa Foster was gray-haired but otherwise looked like a girl out of the 1920s.

Stan said, "What do you do when you have clients from Spain?"

"What's that?" Ian asked.

"Abdullah."

"Oh dear," Pippa said. "Has he started on that again?"

Ian said, "Fortunately it's never happened. Suppose I'd tell them to say they were from South America."

They got into the landrover once more and drove far out into the country. Stan felt for the first time that he had finished with the plane flight and the sense of disorientation. But he couldn't get over the way the place looked. If it weren't for the animals, the slanting, trapezoidal shapes of some of the trees and the clear, dazzling air, it might almost have been somewhere like Florida.

They tested the guns. Ian was impressed by Stan's marksmanship and Millie was about to tell him: yes, Stan even had medals for it, when she stopped herself.

A car drove up while they were still adjusting sights. Nicholas got out and came over. He told Ian that he'd heard from the Whiteacres, who now thought they would definitely be arriving in a week's time. Did Ian want to wait that long or go on alone?

"There's an even chance that that week is only an estimate," Ian told him. "They'll let you know in another week that they've changed their minds again."

"Makes it awkward for the boys," Nicholas said. "They don't know where they are."

"Well, we've got their money, and they were meant to arrive last week. Tell them we started charging them field rates from the date they originally gave us. They won't miss it."

"But it might aggravate them enough to send them somewhere else."

"They're more trouble than they're worth, Nick."

"Not if they're prepared to pay those prices. We don't have a choice."

Stan and Millie were standing too close to be completely outside the conversation, but made it appear that their attention was directed somewhere else. He checked the sights on a rifle and aimed, lifting the stock to his shoulder and squinting down the barrel. She looked closely at her shotgun as if she might be expecting to find a message printed on it.

"We'll have to get out and back in time for the Rawlinsons," Ian said. "They're regulars and they're punctual."

"We can't afford to lose the Whiteacres, Ian."

"We won't lose them. They've paid."

"They've only paid a part of what it'll come to once we add the extras. And they could do all that with another firm. We've given our word about the work – we'll have to pay the boys."

"What other firm would take them on if we send out the story?"

"Perhaps. G & T would do it."

"Of course. Worst safety record in the business. It's not a question of one hunter and a tent – they'll want a large outfit. Well. We'll leave on the right date and meet you. Stop for lunch. We'll draw up a plan."

Nicholas couldn't stay. He said something about later that night. As he left, he waved to the Binsteads. Stan nodded, Millie lifted her hand and smiled.

Ian began the shooting lesson. Stan offered to show Millie himself, but was told that this was one of those activities, like driving a car, where the husband made a worse teacher than anyone else.

On their way back to the bungalow, Stan asked about the farm.

"You've heard about the ground-nut scheme?" Ian said. "A fiasco. I was in on that. A lot of us were. It's mostly coffee here, but that hasn't been too successful recently. Terrible thing, the weather."

Stan wished that he hadn't asked.

"Friend of mine went into flowers, grows daffodils. Pops them on a plane, they're in London before you know it, all over the world. Coining money. If I'd thought of it at the time – but, you know how it is: one doesn't. And then it's better to see the thing through than pull out and change. That might be the wrong moment, too. Thought he was a bloody fool at the time. Now he's laughing."

"Everything's risky nowadays, I guess," Stan said.

"That's it. We thought we'd made the last big decision in our lives when we opted to stay on. But nothing's certain."

"It never was," Millie said. "That's the way life has always been, hasn't it? Businesses can go broke, countries can go broke, fashions change, politics change. That's what life is: movement."

Ian chuckled. Stan was astounded. The speech, even the fact that she had spoken at all, was so unlike her.

She added, "Of course, it's always nicer when things go well. I hope it picks up for you soon."

"Thank you," Ian said. "We've given the children a start, at all events. That's the important thing."

Millie asked about the children. The Fosters had two boys and a girl, all of them grown up now and making their way in the world. The daughter and one of the sons already had children of their own. The other son had been divorced and everyone – even the boy himself – agreed that it was his own fault. But people never took advice, and especially not children.

"Or parents," Millie said, which made Ian laugh again.

Their lunch was simple and pleasant. Pippa said that if the Whiteacres really intended to take their time, she didn't see why she shouldn't go in their place. "Why not?" Ian asked. "There's nothing you can't leave. Come along. You can do those paintings you're always talking about."

"I shall one day, you know."

"Do," Millie told her. "Come with us."

"You see? You owe it to your public," Ian said. "Those are all her paintings over there, you know. I'm constantly being threatened with more. No space left anywhere."

"Let me think about it."

"Don't think. Decide."

Stan said, "That sounds like one of those battalion mottoes."

"It's a family quotation," Pippa explained. "It's what we used to say to the children when they wouldn't make up their minds. We went back to London once when they were small."

"That was frightful. That was when it came to me," Ian said. "Looking up friends, trying to find a job in the city. Hopeless. And all at once I realized that I'd hate it, anyway. I couldn't stick it. Not after this."

"The first thing they looked for in a restaurant," Pippa said, "was the sweet trolley. And all through the meal, they kept their eyes on it. You'd think they would have decided, but no – when the time came, they kept shilly-shallying over their choice."

"Bloody annoying."

"Yes, that wasn't a very good holiday."

"Come with us on this one, then. Make up for past disappointments. All right?"

"All right," she said. She folded her napkin and stood up. "I have two witnesses now, so you can't back out of it."

They had coffee on the screened-in porch. Pippa told Millie what creams and medicines she was going to need, to ward off insects and avoid general infection. She also gave her a few suggestions on where to shop for what in town. Millie asked about the paintings in the house.

"Most of them are mine," Pippa said. "Yes. It's become a mania over the years. I have visions of certain paintings I could do – marvelous, brilliant pictures. That's what keeps me going. And then they never live up to it. Naturally. But some of these are by aunts and uncles. My people were Indian Army and they all painted. And their friends painted. It was the done thing at the time. One of the cousins was quite exceptional – a genuine talent. But he died young, so only a few of his works were left. The other relations lived to a great age. The ones who hadn't the talent. Well, no talent for painting. A talent for growing old."

"How did he die?"

"Who knows? Malaria, cholera, some sort of fever, heatstroke – anything. It's difficult to imagine now that any army could have thrown away its men rather than infringe the dress regulations. Adherence to the rules at all costs. One of my uncles maintained that the troubles in India only began with the telegraph. After that, the politicians at home could issue their silly orders and the men on the spot had to carry them out. But before that, all the instructions came overland or by sea; it took months. By the time one of the idiot dispatches arrived, the local company man had already taken whatever steps were best suited to both sides. Those are his. And this one's mine, but you can see where I had to start over down at the left."

"It's much harder to correct a mistake with watercolors, isn't it?"

"Impossible, really. The speed is part of it. You should have an overall impression of freshness and of capturing the moment and the mood. I'm a convinced believer, but I think it's usually considered the amateur's medium."

They went outdoors to look at the leopard cubs, special pets of the Foster grandchildren, who had gone back to their school in England now that the holidays were over. Millie was enchanted. She bent down and talked to the animals; they rolled over each other to get to her, stood with their paws up against the wire, and mewed.

"Can I pat one of them?" she asked.

"Yes, but be careful."

"I've had injections for everything."

"Yes, my dear, we've all had the shots, but they'll not do you much good if you're scratched by a leopard. They're growing so quickly. Here, I'll show you."

Millie tickled one of the cubs. She said, "I just love them. I'd like to take them home."

"One becomes so attached to pets. I used to think it would get better as I got older, but it's worse, if anything. A zoo in Germany wants them. Might as well. They'll be no use out here now."

"Why not?"

"Too long being fed and cared for. Too much civilization. And the boys wouldn't let them alone for an instant when they were here – that was bad for them as well. Jamie was too ridiculous, said he wanted to name one of them 'Kung Fu' and take him back to school where he'd train him to kill on command."

"I guess the boys will want to come live out here eventually?"

"It would be lovely, of course. A dream come true. But one shouldn't plan ahead. It's too far away."

34

"For me," Millie said, "everything out here is so beautiful to look at. One of those places where you know beforehand that it's going to be perfect, just like the postcards. But it isn't what I'd expected. It's much more. And there's something else. It's a feeling in the air. The air is different here, it gives you such a sense of excitement and space and freedom."

"Yes, yes. That's it."

"You don't like thinking of them being in a zoo, do you?"

"I shouldn't allow myself to think it. It's a sentimentality, for my own sake. It's best for them to go where they can be looked after properly, I know that."

They started back towards the house. Pippa stopped once to put her hand up as a shield above her eyes. She stared off into the distance at a large, heavy, expensive-looking car that was traveling along the road.

*

Stan and Ian talked about the government. They had already discussed Lavalle and the Anthropology Department, and even the renegade Canadian scholar and his forthcoming film. Stan asked about the three officials who had taken charge of him in the morning, and said something about the tension he had felt between them.

"It wasn't really anything I could pin down. They were sort of holding something back among themselves and at the same time trying to outdo each other towards me."

"That puts it nicely. Yes. I think you'll find that all over this part of the country, everywhere, the one thing you must never accuse an African of is tribalism. It makes him furious. It's the one imputation he can't stand. Because, of course, it's usually true. It's also true that it's much more complicated than most

Europeans realize when they use the word, so one can under-stand the indignation."

"Is that what was going on this morning?"

"Absolutely. One or two other scores to settle on top of that, but that's what it was."

"I guess it could have gone the other way, too. They could have tied up all the paperwork, with each one trying not to let anything through that didn't give credit to him."

"Not in your case. They knew you were booked with me and Nick."

"I see. Wheels within wheels."

"Well, it's a small place. We old hands have seen a lot. If something isn't right in town, we know which village to go to, and which old man is the one to complain to."

"Interesting."

"Oh, it's a grand place."

Millie and Pippa walked towards them from around the corner of the veranda. The car in the distance came nearer, driving up to the house. Two men alighted from it and were introduced to the Binsteads as Colonel Armstrong and Dr. Hatchard. The colonel was tall, red-faced, talked in loud barks and had his moustache and sideburns arranged in two large sickles of hair. The doctor was dark, bald, clean-shaven and had muddy-colored eyes. Armstrong began straightaway to ask the Binsteads all about themselves. He skillfully linked his questions into further ones, so that soon Stan was talking about academic backbiting and the risks of publishing, or worse still, not publishing.

"Come to our house tomorrow night," the colonel suddenly announced.

Millie looked at the Fosters, who both gave tiny, almost imperceptible warning movements against the invitation. Stan said that they would only have that one day left and were planning to set out the day after tomorrow, in the morning. Armstrong told him that in that case, they must certainly come, meet all the neighbors.

"Don't tell me Ian isn't having a shauri for you. No? That's no more than I'd expect. Well, well, you'll have to come to ours. Can't have you going off on safari without meeting anyone first."

Stan accepted the invitation and also the offer of a drive back to the hotel.

The men moved towards the porch. Armstrong talked with Ian, while Stan accompanied Hatchard to look at the leopards. Millie stayed behind in the hallway with Pippa.

"Is he always so definite?"

"We call him Colonel Headstrong," Pippa whispered. "His wife's the only one who can keep him under control. It's partly the climate, I think. He's not so bad, really. It's just his way." She gave a shrug and made a little gesture that Millie decided must mean drink. "But his friends –"

"You mean the party?"

"Not our sort of thing. Very loud, very crowded. Hundreds of strangers shrieking at each other, spilling their drinks, wandering off into the shrubbery."

"I don't think I've been to a party like that since I was in my twenties. All I can remember is that they're wonderful for the first hour and a half. The trick is to force yourself to leave early."

"Or not go at all."

The men had stationed themselves at the front. The driver held a door open for the colonel. Millie said, "You are coming on the trip, aren't you? Bring the paints and come. Please."

"I haven't even begun to think how I can leave the house for so long."

"But you're going to?"

Pippa shook her head, laughed a little, and said yes, of course she was coming; life was too short to waste time trying to find excuses for not doing the things you really wanted to do.

They walked out to the car, where Ian stood talking to Stan. The colonel and the doctor were already sitting inside, the colonel in front with his driver, the doctor in the back. Millie and Stan got in with the doctor.

As they moved off, Armstrong said, "Good man, Ian. Known him forever. Knew him when he was a boy, working for Odell."

"Who's Odell?" Stan asked.

"He started the firm. He was one of the grand old men."

A silence followed, into which Millie suddenly said, "Dr. Hatchard, are you related to the author, Rupert Hatchard, who wrote a book called *In My Sights*?"

Armstrong slewed around in his seat, saying, "The lady's read your book, Binkie. Jolly good."

"Then you are?" Millie said.

"Yes. A poor thing, but mine own. Nothing much to it."

"Oh, but I thought it was very good. And lots of wonderful stories, too. I was really scared by the one about the ants."

"Oh, that."

Armstrong laughed. "That's one of Simba Lewis's. Considerably cleaned up, I might add."

"And the one about the flamingoes," Millie continued.

"That one as well, wasn't it?" asked Armstrong.

Hatchard laughed too and said, "Yes. I wouldn't dare put in the originals."

"But won't this man mind if you use his stories?"

"No, everyone here knows. And I asked him. 'Right you are,' he told me, 'clean it up and bung it in, two per cent of the advance – cash, no tax – and we'll call it a bargain.' "

"Does he write any books himself?"

"Harry Lewis?"

"They wouldn't print it if he did," Armstrong said. "Remember that letter he sent to the papers?"

"And I liked the title," Millie said.

Stan thought: *Somebody else probably wrote the title, too.*

"Are you working on another book?"

"Well, yes. I had thought of it. The first one went so well, the publishers asked for another. This one's mainly about elephant."

"That sounds good. Do you have a title yet?"

"No, I've thought of several, but can't settle on one. Any suggestions?"

Millie said, "Well, I can only think of one, but I'm sure it's been used before, because it's so obvious. You could just call it *They Never Forget,* or something like that."

Armstrong said, "That's not bad."

"I won't ask for two per cent," she added. The two men laughed loudly. During the rest of the ride, she talked about her trip through the game park. Armstrong planned a similar excursion for Stan the next day; he was peremptory. Stan had to acquiesce.

They said goodbye at the hotel entrance. Millie waved, Stan gave a kind of casual salute and turned around. He said, "What do you want to do? I'm still flaked out from the plane." He yawned.

"We haven't seen all the town yet. It would be a shame to miss it if we're going to be leaving, day after tomorrow. Let's explore."

He would rather have taken a short nap, but this wasn't like London; here she really would feel lost wandering around alone.

"All right."

"And we could try some fancy place for supper. How's the money holding out?"

"Oh, it's all right."

"Eat things we aren't going to be able to get when we're out in the wilds."

They walked without heading anywhere in particular and looked at all the extraordinary things that they'd have taken for granted if they hadn't been tourists. Millie's eye was caught by a row of blue-flowered bushes that grew on the traffic islands in the middle of the street. Everywhere there was something worth noticing; a man in the distance walked by with a monkey sitting on his shoulder, and she turned her head as two boys passed, one covered with red dye and wearing a black cloak. His friend carried a spear.

Stan said, "What got into you there? That repulsive man – gushing over his book. 'What a wonderful title.' It sounds like just a lot of rewritten anecdotes other people told him."

"No, it begins with a long chapter on the nature of sight and vision. He's an eye doctor. And it isn't that he's repulsive at all. He's just very lonely, almost suicidal. I bet the colonel is practically the only friend he has."

"What did you do, pick all this up on some kind of ESP broadcast?"

"Why did you accept the invitation if you felt like that? Couldn't you see the Fosters warning us away?"

"Was that what it was? I thought there was something. Well, the colonel seemed all right. He was the one who was offering."

"The colonel's a windbag, but kind of a sentimental old thing, I expect, underneath all that haw-haw-haw act."

"Wow, you're really coming out with them today, aren't you? I thought Pippa Foster was nice, anyway."

"Very nice. One of the nicest people I've met."

Stan was moved and vaguely upset. She had never expressed herself like this before. She had never expressed anything. Suddenly she was giving out judgments. It amused him a little, but at the same time almost made him feel nervous.

They stopped by a camera shop. He looked in at the ranks of photographic equipment. "That's a thought," he said. "You didn't even bother to bring your camera, did you? All we've got is my old one."

"I told you. I want to look. I don't really want to shoot."

"This is cameras, Millie, not elephant guns."

"Same thing. Once you shoot it, it's dead."

"Right, that gets rid of quite a lot of twentieth-century culture."

"I don't mean movies. They're meant to be fake. They're like the theater. I mean – when you look at something, that's real. When you take a picture of it, that's an interpretation. Like keeping a diary. It's a distortion of reality one stage beyond the natural one."

"What about documentaries?"

"No such thing. Impossible."

"Oh, really. Well, that's interesting." He almost said he wondered what Jack would have to say to that. She would wonder, too. And why he hadn't introduced them straight-away. Of course it was understandable why he hadn't wanted to do it after his first meeting with Jack, but perhaps right from the beginning he'd had some idea what might happen. Maybe he'd wanted it to. That kind of thing probably went on a lot. You never thought about some corners of your own world until you had experience of them or knew people who lived that way. And, after all, it hadn't been so different from what used to occur in many countries during fertility rituals. In some places it was still part of the culture.

She said, "Don't you remember that documentary about the insane asylum?" He had taken her to see it at a time when she was beginning to think she might be ready to go out of her mind herself. "What do you think that showed? A true assess-ment? I thought it was about what was in that man's head. The one who made the picture."

They walked on. She said, "Anyway, I never remember things I've photographed. Once I've got it, I only remember the photograph. It's like losing the real thing."

He sighed. He glanced sideways at her, but she was looking straight ahead, relaxed and alert to the sights in front of her. She had already picked up a touch of the sun and it looked good on her.

Everything should have been fine in this beautiful place and on this splendid day, especially when for the first time in years his wife was returning to a state approaching normal life, but as they moved forward, all at once he was gripped by a sense of dread that took the strength out of his legs and made him feel sick all over.

He had never known anything like it. It went almost as quickly as the time it took to notice it. He was seized, made faint, and emptied as though he'd just thrown up. Then, the instant was gone. And he was the same again.

He was sure it had nothing to do with his heart or his lungs or anything. The attack had just seemed to rush at him from outside, like the sky dropping on top of him. It was one of the weirdest things he had ever been through; like an hallucination – utterly convincing, and the next moment not a trace there. All that remained was the knowledge that something terrible had come close to him, pushed him to the edge of endurance, and then gone away. It had been so bad for just those few seconds that it had seemed to take from him the capacity to fight back, even to react against it in any way. He had almost doubted his ability to keep breathing.

"Have you forgotten something?" Millie asked.

He had gradually slowed down and come to a standstill.

"No ..." he said, and then wondered whether it might be because of the stuff they had all taken in London – whether this was some kind of after-effect. But now that it had passed, he felt all right, only troubled by the question of what the cause could be. It couldn't really be the altitude either, or changes in the air pressure.

Millie waited beside him. He stared ahead down the street full of movement and light. She gazed absent-mindedly into the windows next to her. Suddenly she raised her eyes. A man inside the shop, who had been facing out in her direction, lifted his head evidently at the same time, and she found herself looking straight at him, intently. He had a strong face:

dark, gray-brown eyes set under straight eyebrows, cheek-bones that stood out, a short, irregular nose, over the bridge of which there was a small scar, and there was another tiny mark near his upper lip. He had a two-day stubble on his cheeks and thick, ragged brown hair that grew back away from his forehead. He was wearing an open-necked khaki shirt that had a tear in it near the breast pocket.

She felt the top of her head go light and seemed to forget where she was. It was peculiar to be looking directly into some-one else's face, with nothing but a pane of glass in between. They were actually near enough – if it hadn't been for the inter-vening window – to kiss each other by just leaning forward. The man smiled. And she smiled back, without any strain or embarrassment. She felt that they knew each other now. And she thought that she'd fallen in love with him a little.

"Let's go that way," Stan said. He took her elbow and wheeled her away, started walking, and pointed down the street.

She half-turned her head as though to look back, but then didn't. They were too near the windows for her to be able to see anything unless she twisted all the way around. Stan was stepping forward with a jerky quickness unlike his usual easy lope. Strips of sunlight alternated with squares of shade from the awnings. They walked across an open space and she took out a pair of sunglasses from her handbag and put them on. He said he was feeling the lack of exercise; he wondered if he could ask the hotel where he could play a game of squash.

"I'm sure they could find you a tennis court," she told him. "And they've already got a swimming pool."

"That's right. I forgot about that."

What would you do without me? she thought. She'd never say it. Once at a party back home, they had heard their friend Sally Murchison ask her husband, Jerry, what he'd do without her and he had answered, "Rejoice."

They passed under an overgrown archway into a small botanical garden, went through to the other side and after a while found several streets full of Indian shops, where Millie looked at miniature painted animals for her nieces and nephews. The toys were all just like the ones she could have bought in London. The type of animal, as well as the workmanship, was Indian, not African. Stan thought it would confuse the kids.

They found the museum he had been searching for. He set off straight for the paleontology department he was interested in and left her standing in a corridor. A group of schoolchildren cut her off and after that she spent some time examining insects in glass cases. There was another section on birds, but she hurried through them in order to make sure of meeting Stan. And then she couldn't find him.

In the end, she waited outside and he took twenty minutes to come out.

"I thought you were right behind me," he said.

"Interesting?"

"Yes, fascinating." He began to talk. They walked back to the hotel slowly, her arm linked in his. She realized that he was more comfortable now.

He talked on. He thought that maybe things weren't going to be so bad after all, especially if Pippa Foster was going to be along on the trip to give Millie some way of spending her time.

At the hotel, they asked about a restaurant, changed, and went out for their evening meal. Millie said later that the people at the other tables had almost distracted her from the delicious food. They heard French, German, Italian and Chinese from their immediate neighborhood, and there were obviously more languages from other nationalities in the two rooms they walked through to get to their table. In one of the German-speaking parties near them a woman was dressed in some kind of couturier creation: a low-backed, shoulder-strapped gown that curved out into a full-length skirt of lilac watered silk.

As soon as they were seated, Millie whispered, "I wish I'd had the nerve to go for something like that in London. Something really bright, instead of restrained good taste."

"It would look silly."

"No, it wouldn't. It looks great. It looks terrific."

"No, it doesn't. It's inappropriate."

"It's only inappropriate in a way that makes you wish everybody in the room had dressed up like that. A dress like that makes its own occasion."

"You sound like fifty wise sayings from Coco Chanel. A dress like that is an anachronism."

"I don't understand what you're talking about. The study of paleontology is an anachronism."

Stan said, "Look, Millie, a study of the past is not the same as a fashion that's out of date."

"This fashion may be just coming back. You may not have read the right magazines. This woman may be the ace trendsetter of a jet-set you've never even heard of. She may at this very moment have a bluebird tattooed on her instep."

He started to say something else, when he realized that she was joking, and enjoying herself.

They skipped the dancing, which was still going on at the hotel when they returned, and made it an early night. That was what Stan called it; early to sleep, rather than early to bed. In the morning he showered and dressed quickly, before Millie was up.

They passed each other at the reception desk as she was on her way to the dining room for breakfast and he was waiting for Colonel Armstrong's driver.

"Have a nice time," she said.

*

Over breakfast she made friends with an old woman named Miller, whose son was doing research on sleeping sickness. Mrs. Miller walked with a cane and had dropped a large hand-bag on entering the room. Millie, right behind her, had retrieved it and suggested that they sit together, since her husband had had to leave early.

"Unless your family –"

"Oh no, that's quite all right. My son is going to visit me for tea later today. By all means let's sit together. How kind of you to suggest it."

The rescued bag contained a great deal of knitting – for the most part children's sweaters in fine yarn and crisscrossed by complicated designs. Mrs. Miller mentioned grandchildren.

Millie wondered why the son wasn't offering his mother a place to stay. She even asked if there was a daughter-in-law and was told yes, but always very busy, poor thing. So, either the younger woman didn't want Mama horning in on their life, or perhaps the son himself didn't. The old woman was so placid when she spoke of her relatives that it was hard to tell what she was thinking, nor did she act like someone on vacation. Millie suddenly imagined that she might have come out to the country without warning, because she had found out she was ill or dying and didn't want to be alone.

They talked about Africa, about the weather and trees and flowers, what they'd seen so far, and about knitting. They introduced themselves. And Mrs. Miller told a story about a cat she had once owned, that could do tricks without being taught. It used to scramble up the curtains and hang there upside-down in order to tease her. She said that even here, or especially here, one was aware of the insoluble bond between man and animal.

"Man and the plant world too, of course. We all live on the same earth."

"Yes," Millie said, "and we sometimes seem to take on each other's characteristics, it's true."

Mrs. Miller leaned forward. She said, "The planet, I am firmly convinced, is a single cell. Otherwise, it doesn't make sense. Any of it. Indeed, the universe itself is *one.* Hence the name, universe." She spoke the last phrase with an air of great seriousness, like a player on the stage who is about to reveal the secret of the lost treasure or the real name of the criminal mastermind.

Millie smiled. She handed Mrs. Miller the sugar and said she'd never thought of it that way before, but it was an interesting idea.

*

After breakfast, she went for a walk. She looked in store windows, passed on, returned down the other side of the street and worked her way through the modern business section of town and into the jumble of Indian shops, where she dawdled over bright displays of scarves, statuettes, rugs, blouses, beaded purses and painted boxes.

She was leaning over a basket full of more small carved wooden animals, when a voice beside her said, "Don't bother with those. They've got better ones down the road." She looked up and again found herself staring straight into the face of the man she had seen the day before, but this time there was no pane of glass between them. He had shaved and was wearing a light summer suit and a white shirt. He smiled.

"Are you with Rollo, or with Ian Foster?" he asked.

"Oh. With Ian Foster."

"Good. You can't go far wrong with Ian. There are a couple of others that are okay, but two of them are out working at the moment. How long do you have in town?"

"We're leaving tomorrow morning."

His expression changed very slightly and only for an instant, then he said, "My name's Henry Lewis. I hope you don't mind my coming up and talking to you. We all know each other here."

It was said in such a way, so naturally and sincerely, that she wasn't angry or annoyed, or even made uneasy.

"Of course not," she said. "My name's Millie Binstead."

"Was that Mildred or Millicent?"

"Actually it was Millamant, but I can hardly believe it myself. It came from my father's favorite play."

"Well, Millie, if you're leaving tomorrow, I can't let you waste your time on this. Come on down the road. You tell me what you want, and I'll show you the best bargains. Or are you just browsing?"

"Oh, a little of both."

They began to walk slowly down the street. Millie felt elated but vaguely dazed, enraptured by the progressive rhythm of warmth and shade. The sound of his voice came to her hardly as part of the exterior world, but as though inspired within herself, like the beat of a second heart. The man was hypnotizing her. She had been aware of the same thing the day before, right through the window. He had a romantic look to him too, but what really captured and magnetized her attention was the fact that he seemed to be obsessed about her. She wasn't shy or flustered. It was strange. It was like what she had said to Pippa Foster about there being something in the air.

"How long have you been here?" she asked him.

"Oh, for years. I'm a professional hunter. Like Ian."

"But you're American?"

"Canadian. I was American a long time ago, then they split up and we moved."

They walked down an alley, turned left and came out into a courtyard. All around, like boxes set between the spokes of a wheel, were small shops. The windows were open, but screens were down to protect the interiors from insects. Up above, all the awnings joined. Only at the very center of the yard the sunlight fell in a splash.

"Look," he said. He took her arm. It was as though they were face to face again, although in fact walking side by side. She could tell where every part of him was, she could see him even though her eyelids were partly lowered.

They went into three or four shops. Everyone knew him. Millie bought five wooden animals, two scarves and two shell and bead ornaments, like belts but without buckles. The owners hadn't wanted her to pay, because she was with him; she had to insist.

They came outside again and turned into a wide street. They hadn't gone far before they were in a crowded marketplace. The first shops had been Indian, these were African and there were groups of children playing on the ground and in and out of the piles of goods. There was also a lot of noise, unlike the well-behaved hush of the places they had left.

A gang of children surrounded them and jounced up and down, singing at them. Lewis laughed. He said, "I shouldn't have brought you through here. I forgot. I'm the man who gives them candy. Wait a minute."

He looked to his right, guided her to a stall, and began to talk to the owner, who flashed out a smile and reached down behind some bolts of cloth for a box at the back. The children kept on singing. They started to dash forward to touch Millie's skirt. Lewis shook his head and growled something at them. They squealed with laughter and then began to chant even harder.

"Is it a game?" she asked.

"They're just being silly."

He turned around from the booth, his hands full of a big collection of colored sweets wrapped up in cellophane. They didn't look like the kind of thing she would have expected to find being sold from an open stall; they were like red and yellow, green, blue and orange jewels in their clear coverings. He shouted out, and tossed them all high up into the air. The children fought to get as many as they could.

"Come on," he said. The two of them ran back the way they had come and walked quickly until they found a quieter street.

He told her, "That's the trouble with small towns. Everybody knows you."

"What were they singing?"

"About you. They were saying, 'O Bwana Simba, what a beautiful bride you have.' They thought you were my girl."

Millie smiled. "That's nice."

"That's very nice," he said. "Well – where can we go? What do you think? We could go anywhere. Do anything. I have a whole week off. Come out to lunch with me?"

"I think my husband's expecting me back."

"Was that the man I saw with you?"

"Yes."

He appeared relieved. He asked her how long she had been married, where she lived, whether she had children. He wanted to know what she had seen so far in Africa. She mentioned the game park, then she spoke of London. She told him about the tiger and the spots at the back of the ears, which he had known about already, but had forgotten. She talked about her visit to the Ethnographic Museum and described its exhibits, including the implement for making toeholds. He burst out laughing.

He said, "When I was a boy, I wanted more than anything to go to the South Seas. It was so cold where we lived. Snow and fir trees, foxes and owls. My mother was fond of painting; not her own – other people's. She took me with her one day on a trip into town. Big deal: the metropolis, excitement. I was old enough not to have to be taken to look at the trains or planes, or ride on the camel, but I think it was motorcycles I was interested in at the time. So, I was sort of mad when I found out I was going to be dragged along to paintings again. I figured I'd go through part of it for show and then just sneak down into the dinosaur rooms. But that changed when I saw the pictures. They were all by Gauguin. It must have been one of the biggest exhibits of his stuff ever put together. They came from everyplace – Paris, New York, Switzerland, from the museums and out of private collections, too. I can't tell you what it did to me. It almost drove me out of my mind. Those colors. It was like what happens to you when you're going really fast, just before you lose your sense of location: when everything is more alive. So, I thought, right – that's where I'm going. But time passes, people die, the money runs out. And so on. In the end, I joined the army. Big mistake. Everybody else was protesting and I actually joined. I had my hand out for the gun: lead me to it. And they did. Hunting, shooting, fishing, surviving – all I was good for. After I got out, I saw this ad for a job as a game warden. Here. I've put more tags on more ears than you'd believe."

"And do you still want to go to the South Seas?"

"Maybe, some day. But I'm pretty much settled down here now. Besides," he said, "why would I want to leave, now I've found you?"

Millie laughed. "This is even better than lunch," she said.

"You think I'm joking."

"And I like it."

They came to a street planted with lines of trees, so that as they walked forward they went from light to dark, again and again.

He said, "I live right near here. Only about two blocks away."

"Oh?"

He stopped. They stood together under the branches of a tree that arched and spread away out over them. It was like being at the bottom of a pool. The rest of the street danced with brightness.

"Would you like to see my etchings?" he said, giving her a big grin.

She laughed with delight.

He said, "On the other hand, it's still kind of early for lunch but I could offer you a cup of tea, or coffee."

She looked back at him without answering. He put his hand on her arm. He opened his mouth to speak, and said nothing, and breathed in. His hand tightened a little.

"Ever since yesterday –" he began.

Millie said, "I'd love a cup of tea."

Stan sat directly behind a wiry man of about his own age: late thirties to early forties. The man was named Carpenter. He worked for the government, not for the tourist board. He had told everyone about safety measures, and disappointed the Frenchwoman who was traveling with them. She was a professional photographer and, like many photographers not working inside actual war zones, dressed in what looked like genuine combat-issue clothes. Stan had thought when he first saw her that she was a very small soldier. She was smoking Gauloises until Carpenter said something to her about a fire risk. Stan was pretty sure the rule had been made up just that minute.

He was in the back seat with a large, proper-looking Dutchwoman and a Japanese who was handsome enough to be a movie star. The car was a heavy-duty vehicle, a cross between a truck, a jeep and a wagon. They were all slightly crushed together inside and the view from where he was sitting wasn't always good. The photographer seemed to believe they should have been given a convertible or a jeep. Stan, however, had been told in London about a member of the television crew whose jeep had been accordioned by some large animal – a rhinoceros or a wild buffalo. And God only knew what an elephant could do to an ordinary car if it concentrated. He was glad they were where they were.

From the beginning it was clear that Carpenter couldn't stand the Frenchwoman. She tried to take loudly snapping pictures into the driver's face and spent a lot of time complaining, mainly because of dust on the lenses. The Japanese asked about rainfall, herd numbers and so on, but Carpenter had trouble understanding his accent. Stan repeated a few of the questions, paraphrased in order not to offend the Japanese, whose English was grammatically faultless and not, in his opinion, difficult to understand. It occurred to him part way through the morning that Carpenter might suffer from impaired hearing: either an ordinary deafness or one caused by constant exposure to gunfire at close range – something the army was fussy about, he remembered, because you could sue them if it got worse.

The Dutchwoman said nothing at first. She appeared pleased to be where she was and looked as respectable and dignified as if she were on a church outing. Stan felt there was an unexpressed sympathy between them until about twenty minutes later, after they had gone over some especially bumpy stretches and swallowed quite a lot of dust from a car ahead. She then began to chatter. As he had expected, she seemed to be a very nice woman, but practically impossible to stem. Information about her friends, family, vacations, poured from her. His replies grew quieter and more perfunctory and she became more animated, laughing and chortling. She turned to the Japanese on her other side. All at once he too went into action: out came his friends, family, vacations as well. The silent understanding had been there all right, but between the two other people, not between Stan and anyone else.

They stopped several times to see lion, elephant, giraffe. All the animals were immensely far away, almost dots. The Frenchwoman made a big production of her work, getting out of the car and setting up tripods every time they came to a halt. While she was busy, the Japanese explained to the Dutchwoman that a friend of his was a photographer and none of that was really necessary. Carpenter kept an eye on everyone and on the neighboring countryside. The driver stared ahead during the breaks, his face still and thoughtful except for an occasional ripple of activity along his jaw muscles that showed he was chewing something.

They drove in among zebra and a herd of animals which were larger than ordinary gazelle and had dramatically back-slanted horns. Stan felt caught by the grace of movement as he watched a long outer swale lift itself up from the main body to get out of the way, all its members jumping in accord. The driver was using the car to buzz them. It wasn't blatant and they never left the road completely; nevertheless, that was what he was doing. The herd swerved and an entire wedge-like section of it leapt over to the side in high, far-aiming arcs, right at the three-quarter mark of which the gazelles kicked their hind legs like rabbits. It was fun to see. It also made Stan think about what ability enabled them to wheel and leap together so exactly. It was almost like watching a flock of birds. Men did it too, but only on the parade ground. When he'd gone through his short spell of that, he'd just thought of it as marching. The official name for the whole process was *Basic Training*.

On their way back, the Frenchwoman started a quarrel. She was championed, without having looked for it, by the Japanese. The Dutchwoman came to attention.

"What?" she said. "Excuse me?"

Carpenter leaned over the seat and away from the French being discharged at his head.

"We had some trouble here a few days ago."

"You, personally?" Stan asked.

"No. A few bloody stupid fools got out of their car when they'd been warned not to. It's usually the photographers," he said, raising his voice.

"We will guarantee to stay in the car," the Japanese told him.

"Yes, indeed," the Dutchwoman agreed.

Stan asked, "What happened?"

"Lion. Went for one of the cars. Don't know why. Took a swipe at the window – from above, you understand, on the roof. They hadn't even shut the windows. Laid a man's arm open. Then one of them panicked, I think. Got out and ran. Of course, he didn't stand a chance. The driver had to go after them, and then he was mauled. Damn shame."

"And the lion?"

"Got away. But he's here, somewhere. We tracked him, and he's doubled back."

"Was he hit?"

"Not badly. Enough to slow him down. Enough to make him a nasty customer if he's cornered."

"We will stay in the car," the Dutchwoman promised.

Stan said, "Shouldn't he be asleep at this time of day? I thought lions were nocturnal, they hunted at night."

"By and large. If they're disturbed, you can't tell what they'll do. Can't tell in any case."

"I guess you couldn't have left the body."

Carpenter made a face. "That would have been the sensible thing to do, but of course it was out of the question."

"Leave the body?" the Dutchwoman said. "This poor man

who is killed? What a terrible idea – why leave the body?"

"So the lion would return to it," Stan told her.

"Ah, forget the lion."

Carpenter said, "I'm inclined to agree with you."

"I thought they turned into man-eaters," Stan said. "If they get hurt, or crippled."

"Oh, a few bites out of a tourist, we don't count that. It's the wound that makes the difference."

In the end, Carpenter gave in. They took the route that went past the place where the accident had happened. And there, in what they were later told was the identical spot, a large dark-blue four-door car stood empty, with all the doors open. Carpenter began to mutter oaths. He said something to the driver and then announced, "I'm going out, but if one of you moves from here, I refuse to be responsible."

As he left, taking his rifle with him, he bent down and said, "Binstead, keep the lady in the car."

The Frenchwoman reached for the door handle straight-away. Stan lunged across the seat and put his arm over hers. He said in French that he regretted very much – but. She told him not to be absurd. Would she, he asked her, want her nice camera to be eaten up by the ferocious animals? She said he spoke French like a Spanish cow, and she darted towards the door again. This time he grabbed her by the back of her shirt collar and pulled, saying that he had been entrusted with a sacred duty to protect the beautiful ladies, and it was a matter of honor. "Imbecile," she screamed, "imbecile," and then laughed. He let go. She turned, still laughing, to look at him.

The driver had sat through the whole proceeding without making any movement or sound, not even munching on the thing in his mouth.

Stan said, in English, that if she could shoot her pictures from where they were – through the glass – that might work. She answered in English that she had everything she needed for it, but couldn't she put her head out of the window with the camera?

"Better not. Remember that lion on the roof. When these things happen, it's always very fast. And you aren't expecting it."

"Okay," she said. Behind her, the Japanese had already pulled out a camera of his own and started it whirring.

From then on, as Stan had said, things did happen very fast. They saw Carpenter off in the distance, and another man walking slowly towards him. The two stood together, then both went over to the right and parted again in order to cover a patch of low-growing bushes. They began to move farther and farther away.

And then, there was a rushing. The figures were so small that it was hard to tell at first what it was. But the next moment, leaning forward past the Dutchwoman, Stan realized that what he was seeing was a running woman who fell and writhed around on the ground. There were shots and he saw a lion run back into the undergrowth. That was what had made the woman fall down: the lion had jumped on her from behind while she was trying to escape. They heard the shots distinctly and they heard, even from such a long way and with the windows partly closed, the tiny screaming, quickly lost in the great spaces beyond.

It's the way it must have been in the war, he thought. *The way it must have been the day he died. And they buried him out there.*

Later, when Carpenter talked about it, Stan pieced together what had actually taken place. Many of the things he had as-sumed, were not there. The lion, for instance, was a lioness and had not jumped, but had run along behind and then beside the woman, and brought her down by clawing up at her legs.

The woman was a German children's nurse, employed to look after a child of seven. She had been wearing white – a suit for a European summer, not a regular nurse's uniform – which had made her look so hideously bloodstained after the attack that Carpenter and the other guide were sure she was dead when she hit the ground. But she hung on, moaning and whimpering, to die later in the hospital from shock and loss of blood.

The child, so the survivors said, had been an extremely spoiled and obstreperous little boy. He had declared loudly that if they didn't stop the car, he was going to have to pee on his fellow passengers. The driver had braked, the boy climbed out, and he had immediately skipped off across the grass while the grown-ups yelled at him to come back. The guide started to go out in pursuit, but the nurse brushed him aside. He assumed that the boy would come to her. Of course, she was the one person there whom the child was certain not to obey; he ran on ahead of her, laughing and taunting. All at once they were both far away out on the plain. The guide and driver got out with their rifles, ordering the others to stay put – which they hadn't done.

The boy raced into some bushes and out the opposite side, where he tripped over a lion, two lionesses and five well-grown cubs all lazing in the shade. The nurse followed. She heard what was happening and, since she was higher off the ground than the child had been at his approach, saw part of it. She turned around, running for her life. By that time, most of the car's occupants were over to the right, being shouted at by their guide, and, as soon as he joined the group, Carpenter.

The Frenchwoman filmed everything she could. The Japanese likewise fixed himself in a contorted, knee-bent stance up against the roof in order to get a better angle and he kept his finger on the silver lever of his machine. The Dutchwoman clicked her tongue. She murmured doleful phrases in Dutch, but she didn't look away.

At last Carpenter came back, opened the door and got in. Both cameras were still filming. He spoke to the driver, who started up. They backed away down the track and turned.

At the hotel, Stan invited Carpenter to lunch. Not lunch, he answered, but a drink. They ordered beer in the bar and drank together as Carpenter told the story and added one or two others. He gave the impression that he thought Stan had acted commendably in managing to keep everyone from getting hysterical or leaving the car while the hunt was on. They said goodbye on friendly terms. Stan had the feeling that he had stood up to some kind of test.

The clerk at the reception desk signaled to him as he passed. He handed over a note, which said that Millie had telephoned and she wouldn't be back for lunch but would meet him in the late afternoon at the sporting goods store to collect their clothes and other equipment. He had forgotten all about her.

He had lunch by himself, went back to their room, sat down in a chair and began to shake. He thought about his brother.

*

She came into the shop at about five-thirty. Stan had been there and gone away again. The man behind the counter called his assistant, who took her through into the room where she had had the fitting. She tried on the finished clothes, moved her arms and legs around and checked the seams. Everything was fine. She changed back and emerged into the main part of the store.

"All right?" the assistant asked.

"Yes, perfect. I'll take them with me. Did my husband pay?"

"He said he's coming back. Also he paid, yes."

"Did he say how soon?"

The assistant beckoned. He ushered her to an enormous rattan chair with a back woven in such a way that it stood up like the hood of a cobra. She sat down on the plump cushion and accepted a cup of tea.

Stan found her chatting to two other customers and the three men who worked in the place. She was talking about a government scheme for preserving rare species of animals, but when she saw him she broke off, saying, "There's my husband."

They walked back to the hotel together. He said, "You were the belle of the ball there, weren't you? Holding your salon with a teacup in your hand."

"That was nice of them."

"And what a chair. You could be Fu Manchu's daughter in a chair like that."

"In a chair like that, I could be Fu Manchu's grandmother. Are we going to be late?"

"No. Why?"

"You're rushing off so fast. Didn't you get any exercise today?"

He slowed down. He hadn't realized that he had been forging ahead along the street. He still felt thrown off balance by the sight of her sitting in the strange, throne-like piece of furniture, with a crowd of people paying court to her. And she had looked so pretty. He hadn't recognized her at first.

"I swam some, earlier. After lunch. Before I came to meet you. Where did you have lunch?"

"Oh, a little place somewhere."

"What was it like?"

"Oh, nice. Sort of Indian stew with vegetables."

"You should be careful where you eat in a country like this."

"Think I'll suddenly find a human arm on the plate?"

"I'd be more worried about parasites or one of those venereal diseases that don't respond to penicillin. Half the population –"

"Okay, I feel wonderful now. You can stop. How was your tour?"

He told her about the trip and about the nurse and her charge.

"How horrible. God. Is she going to be all right?"

"I heard she died later in the hospital."

"And the little boy?"

"Well, that's almost too gruesome to talk about. He was sort of divided up."

"Right. I don't want to hear the rest."

"They found his shoes. With his feet –"

"I said I didn't want to hear all that."

"It's been quite a day. Carpenter told me in the bar that the first death they had there may not have been as straightforward as they thought at the time. There's some question now about whether the man panicked at all, or whether he was thrown out of the car by the other people in it. The driver seems to have his own story to tell. But the other passengers deny it."

"These Jacobean death-scenes," Millie said. "Terror by daylight, people grabbed by the throat. It sounds like you got the full tour, Stan."

"Yes. It didn't look much like melodrama to me, though. It looked like war. I guess it's a lot less grisly than a good set of U.S. statistics for car crashes. I was only getting the old-style version, that's all."

Millie thought: *He's started on that again, his brother killed in the war and he himself alive because of being out in Hawaii at a desk job and surfboarding in his free time. But this thing is nothing to do with war, which is all pushbuttons nowadays anyway, and spraying the trees. It was only the blood that made him think that. As if every woman in the world hadn't seen more blood in her lifetime than any number of soldiers ever saw in the field. Only doctors see as much.*

"Let's skip the party," he said. "I'd much rather find a quiet place and have a couple of drinks."

"Oh, but we can't. Not after accepting."

"I don't see why not. We're leaving at the crack of dawn tomorrow."

"What are you going to say – you've got a splitting headache?"

He moved his neck and shoulder evasively and she realized instantly that he must have been thinking just that, but of course he would have planned to say that she was the one who had the headache – like the time, early in their marriage, when he had come home forty minutes late to pick her up for a party and then excused himself to their hosts on the grounds that she had taken so long to decide which dress to wear.

"Okay," she said, "you do what you want to. I'm going to the party. We'll have the quiet dinner and drinks first, and then I can make your apologies when I arrive. Somebody's sure to be able to give me a ride home. Or I could call a cab."

"No," Stan said, "no, I don't want you to go all alone."

"Why not?"

"Well, it wouldn't be much fun for you, would it?" He couldn't imagine her going out to a party alone if he stayed behind. It was the first time she had suggested such a thing. Of course, she had gone out in the evening in London, but that was different. At a party, you had to talk to people. Then he thought: *Armstrong and that eye doctor who wrote the book – she got along with both of them like a house on fire.* A kind of dizziness moved across his senses, left and came again, sliding away and washing back over him. She shouldn't be this way. She never was before. It had started in London. While all that other business was beginning for him.

"Who knows?" Millie said. "I might meet somebody. At any rate, I'm certainly going to put in an appearance."

"Oh, all right. We'll go to the party."

"Don't come if you don't want to."

"Of course I'll come."

They ate at the hotel and completed the arrangements for their early start the next morning. Millie did some more of the packing. She changed into one of her London dresses.

"This isn't a first night at the opera or anything," he told her.

"I bet they'll be all dressed up."

"I bet they're in bush jackets and hiking boots."

"The women, too?"

"Sure."

"But you'll be wearing a suit, won't you?"

"Oh, yes. I just thought – that thing looks so formal. All the way down to the floor."

"That woman last night – her dress was floor-length."

"Well, she was a foreigner."

Millie laughed. "What am I?" she asked.

*

At the front entrance of the hotel she recognized Mrs. Miller, who was standing all by herself, looking out into the street. Millie asked, "Can we give you a lift anywhere?" and she answered, "Oh, thank you, but my son is coming for me." Millie said they were setting out early the next morning, so this would be goodbye. She shook hands and introduced Stan. Mrs. Miller admired the long dress.

"See?" Millie said to him as they got into the taxi.

As it turned out, not only was the party full of women wearing long dresses and jewelry, but several of the men were in evening clothes, too. Millie looked for Henry as soon as they came in the door, and saw that if he had arrived already he must be at the other side of the front hallway. It was a very large house. Every room was a step up, or down two steps, or at some level that varied from each neighboring floor. The basic structure of the building was a square around an enclosed garden, but that was just the beginning. A babble of voices came from many directions, all the different wings of the house.

The colonel welcomed them loudly and with gusto. He introduced them to a redhead of Wagnerian girth and with the pleased, wide-open eyes and shy smile of a child: his wife, the one who could keep him under control. Her name was Rita. Millie fell into talk with her, spoke of London and asked about the outside garden, which they hadn't been able to see too clearly as they drove up. She listened to information about shrubs and plants, while Armstrong steered Stan into a group of men who could tell him any amount of stories about lion, if that was what he wanted.

Mrs. Armstrong delved into the crowd in order to carry out her duties as hostess. She brought two couples out of the teeming congregation of guests, like a gundog going in after the fallen birds, and slotted them into two different small groups. Millie was joined by Rupert Hatchard. She heard more about the elephant book. And she saw the woman who had been in the lilac dress, this time wearing pink and silver brocade.

There could be no hope that Rupert would introduce anyone. He was a man on his own, who had no aptitude for mixing with strangers. Millie settled down for a long talk with him. She learned that he had a wife at home who was an invalid – she had had a bad fall from a horse seven years before; the accident had left her paralyzed from the waist down. She typed his books and helped with the editing. And she kept herself active in many ways. Sometimes she would come to parties, but she hadn't felt like it that night.

As fresh loads of people arrived, the two of them went with the current that swept into the adjoining room. One of the white-jacketed waiters approached Millie and said a gentleman had a message. She looked at the tray he was carrying, which held only drinks, no message, and realized that she was meant to go with him.

"Will you excuse me for a minute?" she said. The waiter led her inwards, towards the courtyard. She couldn't understand how Stan had managed to work his way through so many rooms in such a short time.

They went around two corners. The man opened a door into a hallway. There were no guests here. Even the sound of the party was almost completely blocked out. He kept going. Now she knew it had to be Henry.

The next time the waiter opened a door, he stood back to let her enter, closing it after her.

Henry stood up from where he'd been sitting on the bed and said, "What a wonderful dress."

She turned all the way around and ended in a fast twist, which let the skirt fan out.

He said, "I was looking for you everywhere."

"If you couldn't find me, how did he know who I was?"

"Oh, that's easy. I described you."

"But you didn't know about the dress."

He said, "It wasn't the dress I described."

*

In the room two beyond the larger one into which Rupert had moved with Millie, Stan listened to one anecdote after another about lion. They were the usual tall stories, some of them, he sensed, originally not from East Africa at all, but from South Africa. The men around him seemed prepared to pull his leg indefinitely without becoming openly unpleasant about it. He played along, acting the good sport. Then he told a story himself, which he simply lifted straight from the *Journal of American Folklore.* It was such a hit that the company decided to give up making fun of him. He heard again what Jack had told him back in London – that gangs like the Leopard Men were just criminals, although since the fifties one could also find that they might claim some kind of political position. And, the claim having been made, it would therefore probably be true.

He drank quite a lot. The men spoke of the German nurse and he mentioned that he'd been there – well, not there, but in the back seat and had been told everything by Carpenter. What he'd like to know, he said, was what had happened in the first accident: the one where the lion was on the roof and the man might have been thrown out by the rest of the passengers.

There was a short silence. Three of the others exchanged glances. One of them, named Wilson, said, "Yes, we've been wondering about that. But at this stage, it's only speculation."

"And after that, I guess it's *sub judice*," Stan said. They laughed for a long time, as though he were really one of the boys. Shortly after that, he excused himself from the group.

He walked carefully down the step into the next room, asked a uniformed houseboy how to get to the bathroom, and eventually found it. Just before he reached the sink, he had the sensation of pulling away from himself, as if he were nearly ready to pass out.

He splashed some cold water on his face and thought: *It's because of this morning. I hadn't intended to drink much. And better stop now.*

They had been at the party for an hour and three-quarters. He made up his mind to get Millie and go on back to the hotel.

A waiter sidled up to him as he was wandering from room to room, trying to find her, and asked if he could help.

"Looking for my wife. Time to go home. We've got to leave early tomorrow."

"What does the lady look like?"

Stan described Millie's hair and dress. The man left his side. Not long afterwards, Millie appeared at the other end of the room.

"How are you doing?" she asked.

"Plastered and ready to go home."

"All right. Let's find the Armstrongs."

"Advantage of a New England wife. You may be drunk as a coot, but you thank your hostess." And she would take time the next morning, even in the middle of their departure, to send a note. His parents were devoted to her, so was his sister. They all thought he probably treated her badly in some way they didn't know about. Which he did, of course.

"Lovely evening," Millie said to Rita Armstrong. "It's been so nice to meet you." Stan pumped the colonel's hand, thinking: *He looks a lot more pickled than I feel, so at least I'm not the only one.*

Later that night, Millie heard someone cough. She thought the sound had come from outside. She went to the window and drew back the curtain. The street was still, empty. Then she noticed a shadow near the double line of trees, between the black shapes of trunks and leaves. It moved to the side. He walked out into the open, looking up. He lifted his arms, reaching out to her.

She blew kisses, which she hadn't done since Christmas vacation in her childhood when she used to leave her grandparents at the station.

He held both hands to his heart and made a quick movement outwards, as if throwing something up to her.

They started out so early that it was still dark. And cold. The air was as clear as it would have been right up in the mountains. Stan hardly spoke. He had a slight hangover – nothing really painful and certainly not on the scale he had suffered in London, but something else bothered him, too. He sensed again the dread that had visited him two days before. So far there was merely his own faint misgiving rather than a definite presence; but, even so, it was disagreeable.

He didn't want to think about his brother, or about London, yet now he assumed that this physical oppression had to be connected with a period of his life that had already gone – it was his past catching up with him: all the regrets and anger and moments of bad conscience that he'd pushed away from him at the time in order to get to more unused and untainted life, more pleasures. He would never have associated the feeling with the future. He didn't believe in things like that unless it could be proved that a wish or fear had warped someone's attitude to such a degree that the distortion itself then helped to make an event happen.

They traveled with Ian and his driver, Mahola. The heavy equipment – tents, cooking stores and so on – was in the trucks coming behind them. One other landrover accompanied the cookhouse staff, driven by a man named Mohammed. Pippa would start out later in the morning with Tom and Amos.

It took only a little while to leave the town, leave people, at last to leave all noise. The only sounds proceeded from the engine as they moved forward, and the wheels on ground and undergrowth. Sometimes Mahola turned off the road to take a narrower track that went across the open plain. They saw the shapes of animals moving over the earth before the real daylight began. Figures drew away from them. Once Millie whispered, "Look," and pushed Stan's arm. On her side, near the horizon, a black herd of elephant was outlined against the gray sky. He said, "Like the central hall in the Museum of Natural History."

"This came first."

When the sun started to show itself, it was as if during the night the continent had been under construction, and now the builders had finished putting it together and the curtain was going up. Millie felt at peace. Strength had come back into her, and just as suddenly as this: the sun rose and everything was different. It hadn't ever been this way before, not during the years of her marriage, nor before that, when she'd lived at home with her family. Only now. Nothing threatened her. She had found her life.

Stan slumped towards her until she felt the whole of his weight pressing down and she shifted so that he slid across her lap.

"What a wonderful place," she said, still in the lowered voice they had been using in the dark.

"It's not bad," Ian said. "Not bad."

"It's like the beginning of the world. It makes you wonder how anyone could bear to live anyplace else."

"Wait till we show you the mosquitoes. After we catch one, it takes an hour to get the hide off."

"That part must be a lot easier now, with pills and antibiotics."

"I should say so. Still won't help you if you fall in the river."

"Oh, don't. That was in Rupert's book."

"Rupert?"

"Dr. Hatchard. He said last night I should call him by his first name."

"We've always called him Binkie. I suppose he thought it too – well, it's a silly name. Can't say to a lady: call me Binkie."

"Oh, I don't know. A name's a name."

"They wouldn't agree with you out here. A name can make or break you."

"You mean a kind of description – Dewey looking like the man on top of the wedding cake?"

"Sometimes it's even simpler."

"Oh," Millie said. "Colonel Headstrong."

"Precisely. Got it in one."

Soon after sunrise, the air began to feel warm. They drank coffee and tea and ate soda crackers. Millie caught sight of a strange object up in the air. It looked like a large peppermint. Ian told her, "That's Archie Bell and what's-his-name. His partner. They're carrying out one of their surveys."

"For maps?"

"Ecological maps. They're counting. Just counting the numbers of animals in a herd and in a district. It's easier to keep track of them from the air. You work through the space systematically and don't find yourself going over the same herds twice. Or not at all. Druce, that's his name."

"I've never seen a balloon like it. It looks like a candycane, with those pink and white stripes."

"It's like one of those things in a picture of the World's Fair years ago."

"And it really works?"

"Oh, absolutely. For the forests, it's the only way."

"Have you ever been up in it?"

"Curious you should ask."

Mahola gave a muffled snort of laughter.

Ian said, "Yes, I went up in it once. Not for me. The wind took us and nearly blew us against the mountain. Next day, Pippa insisted on going up. I warned her. I couldn't stop her. Of course it was beautiful weather, clear as crystal, gentle breeze. Only way to travel, she says. But you couldn't get me back in the thing for love nor money."

"It looks like such an easy way to drift along, so lightly. And it would be quiet too, up there, wouldn't it?"

73

"So quiet, the only sound you can hear is your dinner going over the side. I never saw the poetry of it. That's the way it affected her, too. For weeks I heard about the new insight on life and she kept wanting to go again. It's just luck that they're professionals – they haven't the time to give lifts to everyone who wants one."

"They should have some kind of cross-check."

"There's two other teams. We may see all of them. But the others are amateur outfits. One from London – some sort of conservationist group. And the others are Swedes – that is, one Swede and one American. The American's married to a girl who's a doctor, working as a GP. And the Swede has a girlfriend who – I'm not sure quite what she does. Sometimes she follows in the landrover, sometimes she's with the men in the gondola."

"Gondola?"

"That's what they call it. The basket bit."

Stan woke up thirsty when the sun was already fairly high and the day growing hot. He looked at the others, at Millie in particular. It seemed increasingly odd to him – astonishing – that she, who always made a mess of everything, worried, and then made the worrying come true, had not put a foot wrong from the moment she'd found herself in foreign surroundings. Once she was away from home, she said the right words, did the right things, and was accepted by everyone. More than that – they all liked her, very much and straightaway. Whereas he – they tolerated him. And they didn't consider him so interesting or think his academic theory was all that exciting, either. They had undoubtedly seen lots of visiting anthropologists, sociologists, conservationists, and they only trusted the ones who were born there or had chosen to settle down there for life. He had the impression that Hatchard's book, no matter how bad it probably was, would be regarded as a success simply because the doctor was one of them. A better work by an outsider would not be countenanced. Even the archaeologists seemed to agree that whatever you believed should be put into practice. It had to be your occupation, not just thought about. Scholarship was what you stepped on and walked over.

To a certain extent, they were right; it was the only way to find out. Otherwise, why travel thousands of miles, when he could just have used the tapes and translations, and borrowed video material from Jack? He wanted the part of the mystery you couldn't get by sitting at a desk and theorizing. And he was certain there was something in Adler's idea.

*

They went through hilly country with trees, continued on among flatter grassy plains and scrub, and drove through a stretch of land like a desert covered by high anthills that resembled totem poles. They saw a lioness asleep in the crook of a tree. The sky was like the portraits of heaven in the backgrounds of religious paintings: fresh, delicately tinted, unending.

Lunch was sandwiches. They didn't bother to stop. Ian told them about the country as they passed by: how that was where he had taken out a client back in the thirties with Odell and the man had had a clear shot at the biggest kudu buck you'd ever seen, standing still straight in front of them, broadside on, had missed four times and then brought it down by throwing a rock at it and hitting it on the head; how a zebra had gone mad and – totally unprovoked – attacked Rollo Harding's landrover, starting off by kicking in one of the headlamps. Over in that direction ran an ancient elephant walk and beyond the trees there, that was a village – two of the boys came from there.

They made temporary halts, teaming up with Pippa that afternoon, but it took them three days to reach the site of their first camp. During that period, Millie had time to get used to the tents, the washing, cooking and dressing routines, and most of all the idea that at any time they might pick everything up and move on. She loved it all except the washing arrangements.

"You should have been here in the good old days," Pippa told her.

"I know. I've read about them."

"Still, we'll have lovely times when we join GHQ. I saw the plans. It looks like a Hilton hotel. Chemical purifiers, waste-disposal machines that turn everything into heat or electricity, fridges everywhere, generators and batteries. You have no idea."

"It sounds wonderful. I'm still finding it weird enough to be out roughing it with a platoon of people who do all the cooking and cleaning and laundry."

They stayed at the first camp for nearly three weeks. Every day Stan hunted with Ian. They killed antelope for the table and took excursions far out of the area a few times in order to shoot birds.

Sometimes Millie and Pippa went with the men on the hunt; more often they stayed back at the camp or just took a walk and painted, morning and afternoon, with Tom or an older man named Robert. Pippa looked for what she called "a good view" or a singular plant or tree. She worked rapidly and talked at the same time. After the first week, a second folding chair was found for Millie and she was supplied with paints.

The two of them sat a few feet from each other, Pippa concentrated and frowning a little, Millie smiling and absorbed.

She hadn't painted anything since grammar school. And now she made no attempt to reproduce what was in front of her. Her childhood art classes had never taught her that. She could only put down something imaginary.

She made a picture of a large gazelle. She tried hard to remember how the markings went and what size the horns were in relation to the body. Mahola looked at the painting, expressed his wonderment, and kept looking at it in a way so flattering that she gave it to him. The word went around, Ian saw the picture and praised it; everyone did. Millie was persuaded to do more, first another gazelle, then one of giraffe and elephant. She painted a bird standing, a whole flock flying, and a fish. Her masterpiece was a rhinoceros which Ian himself begged her to give him.

Stan, too, said they were nice. "Sort of like Rousseau."

"They should be in oils, but this is fun, too. Pippa's letting me use all the poster paint."

She hadn't been crushed by his comment or read criticism into it as she would have before. She was unconcerned.

*

Day by day the four of them grew closer to each other. Ian and Pippa heard about life in New England and Millie and Stan were gradually introduced to stories about most of the people the Fosters knew or had known in their part of the country; they also learned that Nicholas had a wife named Jill and three small children; and that several months before, Jill had had a complete breakdown and was now in a psychiatric ward. Her mental condition was still so unstable that they weren't letting her out for visits. And the children had had to be taken into care.

One afternoon as they worked at their paintings, Millie asked Pippa, "Was there some special thing that started Jill's trouble?"

"It's so difficult to know. She was a bit scatty sometimes and then she'd cry. Things got to be too much for her. It was as though she lost her nerve. Everyone came to the rescue, but she hasn't been able to get back to where she was. She worried so much about the children. Nicky's been shattered, of course. No idea how to help. Well, she's in hospital now."

"It sounds like ordinary depression. If she can just get through two years from when it started, it should work itself out. The main thing is to take life day by day and keep up with little practical routines. Or maybe it's more serious than that."

"I'm afraid so," Pippa said. She kept painting. Her attack was more like that of a pianist than a painter, the brush in her hand constantly flicking away and dashing back. Millie's approach was slower and altogether more careful.

Pippa said, "A young doctor friend of ours helped with everything. Alistair James. We'll be seeing him soon. He was splendid. We'd had a note from Nick to stop by at the farm, and one of his friends told us she was in there, but there wasn't a sound. We stood outside and shouted, but no one answered. We went in and it was like a tomb. Then the baby started to cry and we found all four of them hiding on the floor of the broom cupboard. All in a heap – buckets and mops and boxes of soap powder and the children staring like owls and holding on to Jill. She was pointing a pistol straight at my head. My dear – she just wasn't there, you know. Completely vacant. I was petrified. But then Alistair said something ordinary about dropping in for a cup of tea and she stood up and came out muttering, 'Nice cup of tea.' And she handed over the gun as meek as a lamb. Well, it's been a dreadful business. And it's not over yet."

"I wouldn't have guessed anything was upsetting Nicholas," Millie said. "He seemed so calm."

"I've often thought it a mistake for him to throw himself into this extra work. And then again, I know it's good to take his mind off his family. Who knows what the solution will be? But he's very tired. Unhappy. Let's hope these Whiteacre people aren't really as horrid as they sound. Ian's had such horrendous reports of them."

"I hope they're even worse," Millie said. "I hope they're revolting. Think of the stories we'll have to tell."

"Not so funny, to be out in the bush with a large crowd of rich boors who've got access to firearms and can't hold their drink. Ian will only stand for so much. He peppered a man with birdshot once. There was no end of a stink about that. I'd rather have a pleasant trip and no story, thank you."

"Not like Stan," Millie said. "Stan says he'd put up with anything if there's a story at the end."

"Even Stan might change his mind if we have to live with it."

*

Stan developed a speckling of small, pink heat-bumps over the backs of his hands and across his shoulders. They quickly spread into a red rash that itched all the time, until Millie said to him, "Stan, you're scratching yourself to death. Let me see that." And she brought out a tube of cream, just like a television actress in a commercial, and cured him within twenty-four hours.

His days began to seem like a summer vacation from long

ago, or dreams of a kind of life he had never lived except on hiking trips. Ian talked a great deal, describing the country as it used to be, and deploring the way it was headed. He told Stan a lot about the Masai and the lion hunts, initiation ceremonies and general beliefs.

"I've read about it," Stan said, "and heard about it from a friend who was doing a documentary for television. But I thought they weren't allowed to have the lion hunt any more."

"No, well that's why one can't learn much from watching the telly."

"They still do? What's it like?"

"The same as it was. It hasn't changed. They go out and drive the lion into an open space. They surround him, make a circle with their shields up on the inside. He's in the middle of the circle. Each man has a spear. They egg him on till he's in a fine old rage – that's not hard. And then the man who's proving himself steps out of the line and into the middle of the circle with the lion. The others close ranks behind him."

"And you've seen it?"

"Oh, yes. Five times in all. The only European I saw who went through it was Simba Lewis. That's how he got his name."

"Tell me about it."

"You're like my boy Davy: 'Tell us about the war, Dad. Tell us again.' Well, there you are with a sort of javelin and a leather shield. Coming at you is your lion, weighing four-fifty to five hundred pounds, has a speed of zero to sixty-five miles per hour in four seconds and on a charge is doing about a hundred and ten. Opinions differ as to what he looks like at that stage, stretched out or bunched up. To me, he looks like a flying rocket even when he's still on the ground coming on. If he's fifteen yards away, you haven't a hope of doing much more than try to raise your shield. When a lion charges home, the speed is so much faster than you'd expected. It's all much more than you expected. You don't know what killer instinct is till you've seen a lion charge. It's terrible. Glorious. Harry said he knew what to do because he'd been taught how to use a harpoon out in Canada. His one worry was that the spear might not be strong enough to take the strain. Binkie was there, too; said he'd shoot the swine if things got out of hand. I don't know how he thought he could help – he'd only got his revolver on him in any case, and even if you had enough gun, what can you do when your man is out there practically locked in the bugger's arms? Well, the idea is that if you can stand up to all that, you must have the qualities of the beast you've conquered. I'm not so sure but what they've got a point."

"Of course they do, if you're being tested for a world where those qualities will be useful."

"Yes, yes. That's going, too. It all went in my lifetime, really. Soon it'll be nothing but dust and poachers, and politicians in the town. The mosquitoes will live through it and the tsetse and the bloody parasites in the water, but precious little else."

*

At times he felt that he was serving an apprenticeship as a professional hunter. He was collecting hints about wind direction and cloud formation, how to read the landscape, how to forecast weather conditions and the presence of game, how to listen. He learned that when you threw out stones to determine where a big cat was hiding in the long grass, a lion would grunt or growl if you hit him, but a leopard wouldn't. All day long, each minute, you had to keep your attention at its peak. Everything was a sign to be interpreted; a different kind of reading from what he was used to. On the day when he shot his first buffalo, he found out for himself that a lot of noise usually meant danger, but so did complete silence: as they went in to get it, all sound ceased. He knew that when the animal broke out upon him, the noise would be tremendous and it would be right on top of him. They made their way forward very slowly, stopping every so often, waiting and listening. He held his breath until he thought he'd burst. And when the moment came, the animal wasn't quite so near as he had imagined, nor coming at him quite so fast, but it did seem to be moving with a massive, undeflectable solidity, like the engine of an oncoming train. He stood up straight and emptied everything he had at it until it knelt down exactly two yards away from his feet and Ian let out a whoop of joy. Stan laughed.

He had begun to understand what had tormented him about the war. The reasons weren't what he had believed. His fear and self-disgust had come from other sources: his brother, the rest of the family. The question of death itself had not caused any trouble. He now knew it was possible and often natural to enjoy killing. A great many men felt the same way; and quite a lot of women too, no doubt. That didn't mean you were a sadist or even that you were cruel, just that if you were out on the hunt, killing made you feel slightly better afterwards rather than slightly worse. You only had to know what you were doing, and why.

Perhaps his attitude to the animals would change if he stayed in the country for a long time. Maybe he'd begin to feel he could leave them alone. And then he might become like Ian and Nicholas, and – even later – think it was a shame to kill. But not yet. He was still intoxicated by the life of the chase and the moment when he sighted along the line, like looking down a road he was going to travel on, seeing a living creature standing there and crossed at the place where it would die.

When you squeezed the trigger, you captured that life. On the instant of being no more, it became yours forever. It really was true, he told himself: when you killed a thing, you became its owner in a way nothing else was ever owned. You equated yourself with the priest making a blood-sacrifice and with the drama released by his act. What was death otherwise, more than the enfeeblement of old age or sickness? Otherwise it had no meaning.

He didn't consider that there was a point of view belonging to the one marked out to die. To kill for food, to kill for fun or an idealistic cause – all were different to the killer. For the victim there was no variety. Dead was dead, just as dirt was dirt, without qualification.

Every once in a while he found himself thinking about his job – the college, lectures, people he worked with. One day the notion came to him that he might not go back. He could even do what that other maverick professor had done, and end up with money instead of scholarly accuracy. When the air was like this, the sky, the health of his body – anything was possible.

He began to become very attached to Pippa and Ian. He felt more at ease with them than with his parents, who were about the same age. And being with them put the idea of his mother and father into his mind. He thought over old parts of his life as though coming to them in a new way. One late afternoon he returned to camp and saw Millie too as if he'd never met her before. For a moment she looked so beautiful that she took his breath away, like some ordinary object that had turned and caught the sun, to become suddenly dazzling, blinding. And yet, she was the same. He had just never seen her like this, not even when they were first married.

He thought: *Well, we'll start all over. We wondered how to get together again and it looks as though it will just happen, like the estrangement itself.*

As he reached out towards her later that night, she drew her arm away from under his hand and told him, "I can't any more," the first time in their marriage that she had ever refused. Sometimes in the past he had suspected or known she hadn't wanted to, but she'd never said so.

He would have to take it easy, fix some time to think about the long talk they had been putting off for years. He was the one who had avoided that, finally. He hadn't been able to face it. They'd never even settled their thoughts on the subject of having children.

When they married he had assumed that she'd want to start a family straightaway. She had no other interests and no other plans. That was the natural thing: he'd go on with his work, she'd take care of the children. Then, they didn't have any. He thought they should go to a doctor. The moment he suggested it, she exploded. She wouldn't go. "You do it," she had told him. He had gone. He was sure he wasn't the one, but as soon as he got to the doctor's office, he felt terrible.

As it turned out, there had been no need. Everything was normal. He was fine. "Shall I make an appointment for your wife?" the doctor had asked. "I think I'd better have a talk with her first," Stan had said. The doctor told him that it could be any one of a number of things, or a combination: a slight infection, a blocked tube, even an allergic reaction to the husband's sperm, or, of course, some psychosomatic change in the metabolism.

"If there's an aversion –"

"On the contrary," Stan had said.

And Millie had asked later, "What for? So we can find out whose fault it is? Never mind. I'm sure it's my fault. Everything always is."

He hadn't wanted to force her to find out, especially since he was seeing someone else at the time; that wouldn't have been right, even though it would have taken her mind off whatever suspicions she might develop. She had been so savage, unreasoning and ugly when he raised the matter again that he didn't know her any more. So, he had left the subject alone. It became a question that got lost with time. But he hung on to his disappointment. And he turned it into an excuse for continuing to be unfaithful: because something was lacking in his marriage, and he had to make up for it. He knew even then that that was the kind of reasoning he was using, but he didn't feel guilty.

Years like that. He hadn't been able to talk to her and she didn't seem capable of picking herself up out of the dark place into which she'd fallen. Yet he never got to the point where he threw it in her face. He never told her that he had been to the doctor.

Now they would have to straighten everything out. That, too. They could keep going the way they were, or they could adopt children. No divorce – he knew now that he had been wrong about that. A divorce was out. At last he was touched. He had fallen in love with her again. And she was right: unless they talked to each other, nothing would ever be any good.

*

The Fosters' friend, Dr. James, who was medical officer of the district, passed through on his way from town, dropped off some mail for them and stayed to gossip. In the middle of cocktails, Millie got up and went back to her tent to bring Pippa a stamp. She picked up her own letters for America and was heading towards the big tent again, when a young man – a stranger in the camp – stepped up to her.

"For you, masaba," he said. He handed her an envelope that had been folded in half and was blank except for her name. She took it, thanked him, and wondered if she should give him something.

"I will take a reply," he said, holding up his hand against payment.

She opened the envelope, saw who it was from, and went back to her tent to read it. She wrote a quick answer.

"Tell him his letter made me very happy," she said to the man. "Are you sure you were given enough for mine, too?"

"Yes, it's my great pleasure I am chosen, an honor to carry your words to him. He's waiting." He rolled up the letter, pinched it down the sides and inserted it into his breast pocket. She thanked him once more and crossed to the dining tent, where she returned to her usual place.

Alistair James sat in one of the extra canvas-backed chairs and held a dry martini in his hand. Pippa said to him, "But how extraordinary, Alistair."

"Not a bit of it. Everyday occurrence. Poor child, she's only just out of medical school. Priceless training, of course, if her nerves can take it. Back there in the so-called civilized countries they don't let one approach anything more complicated than an appendectomy till one's forty. Send them out to the colonies when they're twenty-three and no one gives a damn what you do."

"The colonies," Pippa said. "Really."

"It's still the way they think of us."

"What happened?" Ian asked.

"Oh, she coped. Scalpel in one hand, textbook in the other. No choice."

Millie asked, "What was it?"

"Teenage mother with rickets, been in labor nearly three days. Clearly a Caesarean, but Carrol had never done one. Lovely job, mother and child doing well, Carrol's the star of the show out there. They spat all over her for good luck – revolting custom. I saw her the next day. She was in a dreadful state. Nerves shot to pieces. Everything was all right during the operation, you see, but afterwards she began to realize what it would have been like if things hadn't gone according to plan."

Stan asked some questions about the incidence and distribution of certain illnesses among the population and how they had changed over the past fifty years or so. Alistair spoke of the epidemic of venereal disease and gave it as his opinion that time spent in worrying about the atom bomb was time wasted, when jet travel presented such an unbeatable method of spreading any infection nurtured in overcrowded slums. He then inquired after the Foster grandchildren and the leopard cubs, expressed interest in Stan's theory (towards which he could supply no evidence), and came back to Carrol, who turned out to be the wife of the American amateur balloonist.

"She'll be glad of it later," he said. "My God, what an opportunity. The best hospitals in the world couldn't give one the experience. She's seeing it all. Shame about her husband."

"Oh?" Ian said.

Stan asked, "The one in the balloon?"

"Eddie. And the Swede is Bernhard. Bernhard's all right. A bit of a dreamer."

"Geoffrey said he had his head in the air," Pippa told him.

"And so he does. Eddie's more the practical type. I hope he stays up in the balloon till she finishes her contract."

"Distracting influence, husbands," Stan said.

"Well ... that's not it. It's really Bernhard's girlfriend, a little girl, very wild and excitable. I thought she was a child when I first saw her. She drives along behind them with the provisions and replacements, but what she really likes is going up in the balloon."

"Hear, hear," Pippa said. "I adored my trip. Ian is utterly illogical about the matter."

"Frightful things. Unsafe."

"Quiet and floating. Lovely."

"Float to your death in silence, says satisfied customer."

"Well?" Millie asked.

"You're quick, aren't you? Well. Well, when the little girl goes up in the balloon, it seems they all, all three of them – I don't know if it's some imported Scandinavian custom. Her idea was that she didn't want to be without Bernhard and wasn't going to be, so if Eddie wanted to go, or stay, or join in, he could please himself."

"Oh, my," Ian said. "Another scandal. This is a marvelous country for scandals nowadays. We should have told you."

"Every country is," Pippa said.

"Naturally, he joined in. And now he wants to stay in the balloon all the time. Oh, not quite. He wanted to tell Carrol about it. 'Make an honest break with her,' he said. I talked him out of that, but I don't know. They're so young. Only children, really. It's extraordinary."

"And you're such an old man, Alistair," Pippa laughed.

"Well, older than that."

Stan said that as a matter of fact he thought it sounded great, like cruising around tropical islands in a yacht and making love all the way across the ocean.

"One wouldn't feel comfortable," Ian said. "No. What happens if they're all going at it like the clappers and a breeze slaps them against the hillside? Or down into the trees. Not my idea of romance."

The doctor stayed for lunch. Afterwards he lit a pipe and remembered more news he'd picked up on the grapevine. He also said that he'd had a long meeting with Nicholas at the hospital. And Nicholas certainly had enough on his plate, as the Whiteacres had at last arrived in town, blowing all their trumpets. Everyone had heard about them. Alistair wished the company luck and said they were going to need it.

"I've never seen Nick lose his temper, but how he manages not to with that lot is beyond me."

"I once saw Nicky lose his temper," Pippa said. "His eyes got bluer and bluer, they were like electric lights, and his hair went dark; one minute it was fair, the next minute brown. It was just the perspiration making it wet. No other sign."

"No trouble with the boys?" Ian said.

"I'm sure it's all in the letter. They're having rows. Loud, public – you know. They go out looking for people to use as an audience, then they stage a bigger and better row. They're with an enormous number of other people. And they keep adding more."

"Poor Nick," Pippa said. "Not his sort of crowd at all. As if he hadn't enough worries already."

They walked out into the open to say goodbye. The light around them was like echoes of the sun's heat throwing itself down to the ground. The sky burned from all its edges. Alistair waved and the driver started up the engine. He was the same man who had given Millie her special note.

*

In the evening, Stan leafed through an offprint he'd been sent by a colleague in Philadelphia and Millie read a paperback travel book.

Ian muttered over Nicholas's letter until Pippa took it from him. He asked, "Do you think she'll ever be well?"

"Yes, of course," Pippa said.

"Once people crack –"

"Yes, my dear, I know. That's another one of those Victorian truisms, isn't it?"

"I just don't know what poor old Nick is going to do."

Millie said, "I guess the hardest part is going to be afterwards. When they start to see the effect it's had on the kids. But if they really work together –"

"That's it. How can he drop his work and go look after her for a few years? He can't. It won't be much good wet-nursing her through a breakdown if they have to sell the house and starve."

"And Nicholas has no qualifications for another job?"

"Leave the business? Oh, not Nick. It would kill him. It's his life."

So, Millie thought, *it's the wife, not the job, that's expendable. Just like home.*

Pippa talked about the children. She said that little Elsie was mad about Alistair.

"And about Harry," Ian said. "But a lot of grown women are too, of course."

"She's a prey to infatuations. She falls in love with people. It's rather embarrassing, somehow. A child."

"Maybe she's lucky it comes to her so easily," Millie said. "I've only been in love twice in my life, but some people never stop. And it's pretty much the same at any age, except it means more later. She probably needs attention, that's all."

Twice, Stan thought.

"Well, I'll write to Nick," Pippa said. "Nothing much else one can do. We'll see him soon. Alistair's the one who can tell him what he needs to know."

"The medical part of it," Millie said. "But if a lot was circumstantial, there's another side to it. It sounds like she's an ordinary nice woman except for her condition."

"Oh, she is," said Pippa.

"Except for her condition," Ian repeated.

Millie said to Stan, "You've always told me witch doctors treated the whole case: family, thoughts, job, as well as the bodily ailment, so in some ways they're better doctors."

"Me?" Stan felt himself go numb. It was possible he had once said something like that. He couldn't remember. It seemed to him he had filled years of his life saying useless things to people who looked up to him, or whom he would have liked to convince of his superiority. He hadn't convinced her, though. He had made her unhappy and she'd thought he was contemptible.

Ian said, "Witch doctors. That's a load of old cobblers. They ladle out a bowl of gruel and tell you the guilty man is the only one who'll die of it, and you find out later that's the cup he's put the cyanide in. They're a fly lot."

Pippa held up the top sheet of the letter. "What a time he's having," she said. "I can hardly untangle the cast of characters."

"I'd soon sort them out."

"Yes, that's why I'm glad you're here. It's hard on Nick, but at least he won't send them packing. It'll mean a change of routine," she said to Millie. "He says there might be more people than we'd expected. The Whiteacres are bringing friends."

"Extra friends, extra hunters," said Ian. "If they're planning to shoot."

"Sounds to me as though they won't be in any condition to shoot, probably be staying in the tents all day, sleeping off the night before. Let me see. Two other couples. One young pair, Martha and Bill; they're engaged. Then, a friend of Mr. White-acre's uncle: Otis Stevenson. They ran into each other on the first day in town. He has a girl with him named Darleen."

"No," Stan said. "Impossible. In Africa?"

"She's American. He says she's his secretary. Nicholas says –"

"They're roaring up and down the streets," Ian said, "getting drunk in every decent bar and restaurant in town. It's extraordinary the way people will behave in a country that isn't their own. Extraordinary. Do they think no one sees, no one hears? The whole town is talking about them."

"I suppose they're like people who quarrel in front of the servants and never think every word is going to be repeated to the neighbors."

"Simpler than that," Stan said. "I bet they just don't care."

Ian sighed. "We'll get through it somehow."

Pippa folded up the letter. She said, "Still, I must say, I'm looking forward like mad to the fridges and showers and everything. It's going to be like the Olympic Villages."

"We'll have to call it Fun City," Millie said.

"We may be calling it all sorts of names before long," Ian told her. "Pity things can't stay as they are."

"We can keep on like this, can't we?" Stan asked.

"If they let us. We'll have to see. It depends on the daily shoot."

Millie said, "I liked your friend, Alistair."

"Yes, Alistair's lovely," Pippa said. "We thought he was going to marry a nice girl named Dorcas who was out here two or three years ago. But nothing ever came of it. Just one of those things that didn't happen."

"I got the feeling he was in love with this other doctor, Carrol."

"You thought that, too?"

"And if – Eddie, if Eddie really wants to break with her, maybe the wheels will start to turn."

"That's an idea."

"What's this? Scheming and plotting?" Ian said. "My God, the women in this country are worse than the politicians. The complications they can cook up."

Pippa waved her hand at him. "Back to your paper," she said. "This doesn't concern you. Don't you worry your pretty head."

Millie burst out laughing. Stan raised his eyes and looked at her, but she wouldn't catch his glance.

*

In the middle of the night he woke up and couldn't get back to sleep.

He lay with his eyes open, his arm across his forehead. And he wondered what good his research was doing, if it could be called that. He'd almost forgotten why he had come to Africa in the first place. He had been looking for a story that was being made into a fixed pattern, a standard and order against which to set the chaos of life. But life was for living, not to be studied.

Love, he thought. *We are taught to expect it. When it isn't there, we fall apart. But in nature there is no love, only need. There is play, pleasure, even dreams. But love, as most people understand it: a cherishing of the mind and soul of another being – that's an artificial emotion. Friendship is almost unknown in nature. Family ties prevail over such trivialities. Family ties depend on blood.*

*

They moved camp the next week, staying for a few days at a site which was so much less comfortable than the one they'd left that for a while all of them felt dispirited. The ground was dry and stony, the whole land looked parched and ready for the rainy season. At the other camp, clear blue heavens and juicy foliage had housed them. They had gone north and now it was hotter, the sky seemed almost white most of the time. They breathed in dust when they moved.

Ian took Stan to a village where one of the head elders was an old friend. They talked while Stan stood, then sat, silent. He had learned that, for some reason he couldn't guess, he was not liked by many of the Africans he'd met outside the town. At first he had thought it crude and simple: because he was white, rich (compared to them) and foreign. But then he began to believe it was only because of the way he behaved. He was trying to learn all the rules now, being taught slowly and carefully how to act with people, just as he'd been led to an appreciation of how to adapt himself to the hunting conditions. There was no need to hurry or force the rate of his progress; everything would come at its own pace. Not like his real father: *Speak up there, boy, what do you have to say for yourself?* He wished there had been the time for Ian to teach him the languages, too. It both annoyed and amused him to see Millie so often deep in conversation with Robert and appearing to be communicating fairly easily, whereas all the courses in Swahili that he himself had gone through back home had proved pretty useless – everyone was speaking his own language and dialect.

The old man chatted with Ian, first seriously and then with jokes and laughter. Later, Ian said that it was their usual catching-up talk and they covered all sorts of topics, private and public. Stan understood nothing of the words but felt moved by the sight of the two men and the sound and rhythm of their voices speaking so harmoniously. What good friends they were, he thought. He hadn't had friends like that since high school. Real friends, not like Jack.

At a point about halfway through the conversation, the old man turned to him and asked politely about the important things in his life: his country, his family. Stan liked the diplomatic way in which shock and pity were repressed as he admitted to having no children. He spoke about the hunting and declared that it was good to be able to learn with a teacher like Ian. That was the right thing to say. It pleased the old man. The talk went back out of English again.

On their way home, Ian said that as far as his friend knew, there was no new political or religious movement in the vicinity, nor among other villages he visited or heard news from. "But..."

"Yes?"

"He said something about songs and dances. I expect it's simply the same ones they've always had. He seemed to believe they were new. I don't think it means much, to tell the truth. It may be someone's distortion of – you see, nowadays it might even be that someone's cousin in town saw a film on the box and described it with local additions. Adapted it. He told me a kind of ghost story that might be nothing more than that. How can you tell whether these things are really intended to be anything or to mean anything?"

"That's what we're trained for. And that's the kind of thing I'm looking for. What was this ghost story?"

"A lion that lives among people and then goes back to the pride. But, surely you recognize that – it's the story of Elsa the lioness, isn't it?"

"Did he say the lion was male or female?"

"Male. But that might just have been a twist, to make it more interesting."

"Anything else? Only that one thing, or were there any stories surrounding this figure?"

"He heard it from someone else. That was what he did say: the story doesn't come from this part of the country. Well, we'll go to the someone else and try to track it down. All right? Like working for the police."

"It's like hunting," Stan said, "but a different kind."

*

He started to have bad dreams and there was no reason for it. All day long he was fine, except for the feeling that came over him every once in a while and which was so hard to explain but unmistakable as soon as it happened. It wasn't like tiredness or a suspicion that things were wrong. It was more like an apprehension of horror somewhere, although nothing was to be seen and there was no object or event that could have given rise to it.

One afternoon he took a nap and had a dream that he thought at the time was a good one: he dreamt that he was climbing into a large wicker basket like an enormous picnic hamper. A pretty girl and a young man got in with him. Above them, like the base of a giant rose, spread the swelling shape of a balloon. The man took out a pocket knife and cut a rope at the side. They started to go up. It was like being in an elevator. Then they began to travel horizontally. Stan looked down and saw the tops of trees speeding away from him. The balloon bobbed to left and right in a zigzag path, the air bounced lightly under them a few times, and the movement stopped. They were suspended. Everything was held in a state of abeyance, and silent. Later on, when they drifted high over herds of animals, noises came up to them made very small by distance, yet clearly audible; but right at the beginning, he was impressed with the complete hush and a beauty of motion that seemed effortless, almost without impulse. He felt his heart lift. The young man wrote in a notebook, the girl hummed a song; he wore a striped sailor's jersey, she had on a dress made out of some kind of sparkling material. They were both about the age of Stan's college students. He began to feel very happy and the balloon started to rock gently, like a boat. The young man leaned back against the rigging and said, "This is the life, Stan," and he answered, "This is the life." The girl gave him a big magazine-cover smile, beautiful. She put out her hands and touched him. He woke up with a jump and laughed a little. He felt terrific. But later in the day he remembered how young the two had been – he was really old enough to be their father. And for a few minutes he was overcome by fury and remorse at the thought that he had never had the chance to do anything exciting with his life when he'd been young. Going up in balloons, fooling around with new adventures and experiences – he should have done all that long ago, and finished with it, and moved on.

*

When the next batch of letters arrived, there was another note from Nicholas, to say that the Whiteacres were finally on the road, with every last piece of the tremendous load of stores, machines and baggage. Their four friends were in the safari and it was like being in charge of troop movements.

Pippa handed the letter to Ian when she'd finished with it. "Nick says so far they've been spending most of their time behind their binoculars, spying on lion servicing the pride. Except when the Whiteacres are trying to outshoot each other and coming close to blowing their heads off. It seems Jill's had a bit of a setback, too." She shook her head. "He always says less than he feels."

"He'll be all right," Ian told her.

"How do you know?"

"She's the one who's the problem."

Millie said, "It's too bad she was in such an isolated place."

Ian agreed. "The worry," he said. "The fear. And being alone there when Nick was off on safari. Thinking she had no protection for herself, and certainly wouldn't be able to protect the kids."

"Was she really all alone?"

"Of course not. Dozens of boys working round the house, on the farm."

"Oh, I see. No women to talk to, that kind of thing."

"That's it. No community life. Her kind of community. One other person would have kept her on the rails. It was all right when old Mrs. Hastings was still alive."

"Mad as a hatter," Pippa said.

"But not bad company. Frightfully funny, sometimes. All that makes a difference."

"But this is her home. She grew up here. It isn't a case of some young wife in the foreign service who's never seen a black face. I still think that last baby took something out of her."

"That could be. Not denying it. I don't think it's the only reason."

*

This is crazy, he thought. *I'm not even approaching it the right way. I've hardly taped anything except the sounds of the animals at night. I don't know why I'm still pretending there's a publication in it. It's become something entirely different. I think I'm right on the track of it, and the next minute it slips through my hands and there's nothing. I feel the way I used to when I was a child, obsessed by questions of why we die and where we go afterwards and is there a God, is there a limit to the universe and if so, what's beyond that: if I could only solve the mystery, everything would be perfect.*

"The mystery is about yourself, Stan," Jack had said in London. "It's always about yourself."

And when he woke up in the middle of the night, he seemed to hear an echo saying, "What are you scared of? Afraid you'll like it?"

*

They changed their campsite again, this time finding a lush spot near trees and not far from a small stream. There were large numbers of animals in the vicinity because of the water; they would even wander into camp. And there was a wide range of good views to paint.

On the third day after their arrival, Millie and Pippa saw a green-and-white checked balloon riding low in the sky and coming slowly towards them. They left their paints and ran to meet it. Robert and his friend Odinga went after them, shouting and whipping their arms in the air.

They reached the road and waved. The balloon drifted along as lazily as a leaf on a slow-moving current. One of the men in it gave them a friendly sweep of his arm, the other had a telescope to his eye and wasn't looking in their direction.

"It's the London team," Pippa said. "One of them is English and the other's a New Zealander, I think." Millie stepped forward to begin making her way through the long grass of the field beyond the road.

"Don't go out there," Pippa said sharply. "Anything could be out there."

Millie stopped. "It's just a field," she said.

"It's just a field where at least twenty lion could be snoozing with their cubs, or leopard, or anything. Even a warthog can turn nasty."

Millie continued to look skeptical.

"And the ticks," Pippa added, "and those ants, I told you about them, the sort that leave their heads under one's skin –"

"All right, you've convinced me."

They went back to their paintings. Millie said it was a shame the balloon hadn't landed. It would have been fun.

"More fun to go up in it," Pippa told her. "But Ian's right; they've their work to do. They can't be giving us rides all the time, more's the pity."

"You know them?"

"I met them once, but only to shake hands. They were in a tearing hurry to start off on one of their trips. The other balloon is the one I went up in."

"Not the group-sex love-nest?"

"No, no. Good heavens. The pink-and-white one you saw with Ian the first day out. That's an official one. The government department. It's the one surveying this territory now. There's another one somewhere. We know Archie and Colin best."

"I'm very intrigued by the skyborne eternal triangle."

"Oh my dear, so am I. I'll tell you if I see them."

"What color is their balloon?"

"I'm trying to remember. No, it's gone. I do hate forgetting things. It's happening more and more."

They talked while they worked on their pictures; Pippa about her grandchildren and about the past, when her own children were small and Ian was working for Odell. Millie spoke, when asked, about her family. She thought of them suddenly at a great distance not just of miles but of time. She caught herself thinking about them sometimes as if they had died long ago. The idea struck her as disconcerting, rather than sad.

*

Stan started three different letters to Jack and tore them up.

The fertility rites of a primitive religion were one thing. And deliberately staged erotic games from the big city were another. Of course they were. And of course it had been different, without a doubt; especially at the end. But none of that mattered. *Forget all that* – that was one of Jack's favorite sayings and he was right. What was important was that he and Millie should be able to draw a line across their lives together and move away from the unhappy past.

He went on a two-day hunt with Ian and came back in a good mood. They cleaned up, had a drink and joined Pippa and Millie for the evening meal.

They talked about the game and about how well conservation methods had succeeded in certain areas but not in others; poaching, disease, the amount of rainfall, were all important factors. Ian had a lot to say on the topic of illegal hunting. And Pippa told a long story which didn't follow from the rest of the conversation: about the famous Curse of the Pharaohs, which might really have been a virus similar to one found on the walls of caves in South Africa, or so she had been informed by a friend of hers back in town. The friend had read it somewhere.

"Rubbish," Ian said.

"No, she was very good on the details. I forget how it worked. The virus is carried by bats."

"I thought they all just died normally," Millie said. "More or less. Pneumonia and things."

"That was the bat virus. It took different forms."

Ian threw up his hands. Stan had no fixed opinions about ancient Egypt. He thought that when they were alone later, he would tell Millie he'd missed her while he was away.

Ian said, "Come on. It's time for us to go hang upside-down."

Pippa yawned and Millie stood up. Stan put down the empty glass he'd been holding. They all said goodnight. On the way to the tent, Millie said she felt that they had known the Fosters for a long time. And Stan, not meaning to put it the wrong way around, said, "Did you miss me?"

She hadn't. She said, "We didn't have the time to miss anybody, either of us. You saw all the paintings we did."

"I missed you."

They went inside the tent. He said they'd probably be moving camp again in two days, and after that the next stop would be the Whiteacres.

"Then," he told her, "we go on to the real country."

"This isn't real?"

"This isn't connected with my work."

"Of course. That's the yardstick reality is measured by."

He started to laugh and felt uncertain. Now that it was important to him to know, he'd lost the ability to tell what she was feeling. He used to know and not care. Perhaps she was deriding him.

Her lips shaped a noncommittal smile, her eyes looked nowhere in particular, and not at him.

She was only teasing. She was fond of him again now, but she often found him very silly. And amusing. He no longer got on her nerves. Nothing did any more. And she would be leaving him soon.

"Ian is afraid of illness," she said. "Especially afraid of women becoming ill. It's odd for a man whose life is so concerned with violence and death."

"Maybe that's why."

"Maybe. Nicholas has the same kind of life, but I don't think he'd disapprove of Jill. He probably just feels terrible for her because he can't understand what's happened."

"You think Ian disapproves?"

"Yes. He thinks she should have had the guts to bring up those kids on her own out there and not crack up, because that's what Pippa would have been able to do."

"Yes. And in a way he's right, isn't he?"

"Of course not. People aren't all alike. And speaking as a woman who fended off an induced crack-up for many years, I'm a little sensitive about it."

In all their years of married life, she had never opened her mouth to tell him. Now it was said: *It's your fault.* Induced crack-up. And now that she had spoken, he felt helpless. He had no position prepared and he didn't know how to respond.

He said, "Goodnight," and pulled the covers over himself.

*

Their new camp was in a clearing by a good-sized stand of trees and behind the trees were bushes. A light breeze played through the branches all day long and most of the night. The hours of painting were never without the sound of leaves rustling, touching, blowing against each other.

We're so glad to hear you are having such a good time, Millie read. She thought about her mother, who had tried to be tactful in asking about children. During the first two years of her marriage with Stan, her mother had warned her not to become a baby-machine. Millie's sister, Betty, had had three children right in a row. One summer morning, when she was expecting the fourth, Betty had a long talk with Millie, said she hadn't wanted any of the children, she'd give anything to get rid of this one, and as far as she was concerned they weren't children; they were unwanted pregnancies, all of them, but their mother thought it was the right thing because she wanted other women to be as miserable as she was herself. The first child, Betty said, broke her – because she was married, so there was no reason she could give why she didn't want it. She had thought to begin with that of course they'd have children, but after a few years. Not straightaway. She'd been sure he knew what he was doing – he'd said he did. So, with the second one, it didn't matter. The damage was done. It was too late. One day she would realize that her whole life had been just this: putting up with things she didn't like, because they were forced upon her. All these unwanted pregnancies would grow up and she would never be given the chance or the time, or maybe after such a long wait, the desire for her real, wanted children.

"I despise him. I despise myself," Betty had said. "And if he knew, he'd despise me too. Everybody would."

"I don't despise you," Millie had said. She had put her own hand over her sister's, where it rested on the table. Betty's hand was without response and she stared ahead of her as if waiting, or stationed there by someone else, a statue standing behind a wall.

Even in the early years, Millie's attitude had changed at least three times: longing for children because it would mean she was a success, it would please Stan and keep him to herself; revulsion against the idea of children, thinking that she would then not only be betrayed but also saddled with the offspring of a man who didn't care about her at all; hoping again, because even if she could prevent herself from wishing for love, she needed someone to touch and to hold in her arms.

She had gone to a doctor at the beginning, had had a thorough check-up and been told there was no reason why she shouldn't be able to have children. That meant, of course, that something must be wrong with her mentally. It never occurred to her that a similar examination of her husband might show some physical reason. She didn't want to hear any more from Stan about the subject. For the first time since he'd known her, she had shouted. And, a few years later, at the stage when she was pretending to want children but didn't, she was using two different methods of contraception simultaneously. She only gave them up because he had stopped wanting to make love. He had his hands full outside the house, she knew that well enough.

One day after she'd been to her parents for a visit, her

father drove her home. She had never talked about her marriage and had finally made it plain that she didn't like being questioned. But before dropping her off at the apartment, he had asked, "Millie, are you happy?" Her father, who was so charming and agreeable; and it was just the kind of asinine thing he would say. Was her mother happy?

She didn't talk to Pippa about any of that. It came across her mind like veils, like curtains, sometimes like a form of speech, as though she were talking to herself while her brush outlined antelope and crocodile, elephant and bouquets of flowers copied from the photographs in a seed catalog that had arrived in one of the mail deliveries.

Darling, she wrote. *I think about you all the time, I never stop. I'm waiting and waiting. I love you forever.*

*

Stan and Ian set out in pre-dawn darkness for the village they had been told about. Ian talked nearly the whole way about Nicholas. It seemed probable to Stan that, as Millie had said, Ian blamed Jill; he was ready to find excuses for someone who made a mistake in work – even a stupid or dangerous blunder – but there was no excuse for anyone who made a private mistake, committed an error of emotion or suffered a collapse of psychological strength, a confusion of the personality. He appeared to believe that that was a matter of choice and if you gave in to a failure or a weakness, it was because life was made easier for you that way.

They sat in a shaded hut: circular, roofed, with supporting poles down the sides but no walls. Stan couldn't tell whether the building was unfinished or the walls removable and perhaps put back at night for protection against the cold and the night-hunting predators.

Four other men sat with them, one young, one old, and two middle-aged. The most important man was in his late forties. He had a leisurely, matter-of-fact way of indicating who should speak next, although also a slight air of menace, which might have been unconscious. Maybe it was an effect he had found useful as someone who was in authority over others. It could mean people wouldn't waste his time as much as they might have if he'd had a sympathetic manner.

"Remember, now," Ian said as they went in, "I don't know any of these men. I've only got a sort of letter of recommendation from my friend." He translated.

From the old man: "I heard it said when I was a child that a lion would come into the country one day that had the powers of a witch. I took this to mean a great man who would lead the people in battle, who would make us rich and happy and bring back the health we have lost."

From the young man: "I hear the children singing new stories about the lion. But songs change after a time. The songs I sang with my friends aren't all the same as the songs my father and his friends sang. Some of them were new to us because they were ours, not from our fathers. This is the way new songs are born. First the singers, then the song. These new ones are about the wedding of the lion and the feast of the guests who make welcome for the bridal pair. The songs don't come from my village. They come from the East."

From the middle-aged man who was not heading the talk: "I heard such songs when I was passing through the country near the red rocks. The Bwana knows it. These songs all come from one village. They are not about a lion; they are about a man who is their witch. He kills the lion."

From the leader: "I too have heard the songs, most of the time sung by children, in a few cases by young girls or boys. But I have also heard of men with masks and dressed in lion skins, who hunt elephant and rhino and sell ivory and horn against the law. I have heard these men don't like anyone to talk. They know boys in many villages who will work for them, make money, go to the city, live like a rich man. I've heard last year six boys, who wanted to talk, died."

The leader didn't sum up, or indicate which explanation he thought should be accepted. He had included his own opinion, not pushing it, and that was enough for him. He turned to Stan, having realized without being told, that all this was for his benefit. Or perhaps he had been briefed by Ian's friend in the other village. Stan caught an ironic glint in the man's eyes. *How laughable this is,* the look said. *Food is more important, infectious disease and all other illnesses are more important; doctors, guns, schools, water, the fear of the locusts coming back, of swine fever among the cattle. Or, if this were a search for an enemy – that too would be understandable.*

Stan moved his head in a slight nod. He turned to Ian. "Thanks," he said, "that's fine, if you can find out the name of that village. And say I appreciate it."

Ian asked the name of the village. After that, good manners forced them to stay a while. Ian talked a great deal and drank tea made from some thin, dark shreds that might have been leaves, bark, herbs or even wood. Stan saw that he too was about to be offered some of the drink. He told Ian quickly, "I thought I said it was against my religion to eat or drink anything on these special days."

Ian explained. The men looked at Stan. He tried to appear staunchly religious without seeming unfriendly.

On their way back to camp, he said, "Well it lasted a long time, but that one man was a winner. If I could get my hands on a witch doctor who's building up his own cult – do you know the village?"

"Not well. I've been there with Harry. He uses a lot of boys who come from there. It's a bit off the beaten path."

"Lion country?"

"Absolutely. Not the easiest terrain for shooting, but they're there, right enough. Of course it's fairly wild country. Not like this, where you can run slap into a tourist hotel every fifty miles or so, if you want to. Different breed of wildlife, of people. The nearer you go to the towns – you wouldn't credit what we've cut out of the digestive tract of some of the game we shoot: dolls, cameras, plastic washing-up bowls. Incredible. That's civilization for you."

"Just to settle whether these things might be imported, or a revival. It makes it more interesting if they're connected with something still happening."

Ian began to talk about lion. He said they were like elephant: once the idea took hold of you, no other animal would do. It could cloud your judgment. He went on to tell a story concerning a hunter who had had a partiality for black-maned lion and wouldn't touch anything else, so a friend of his had caught a lion in a net-trap and dyed the mane. The narrative rambled on, longer and more elaborate than a shaggy-dog story.

"Ian, what did they give you in that tea?"

"Well may you ask, my son."

"Are you tight?"

"I'm . . . absolutely blasted. Happens every time. Marvelous stuff, God knows what's in it. Lasts about six hours and then sleepy."

"You feel all right?"

"On top of the world. Like one of those balloons on a very thin rope. Keep bouncing up, straining away from the ground."

That night, Stan was full of the new possibilities for proving his theory. Millie was quiet, listening and occasionally saying, "Yes, yes, that would be interesting."

*

Sometimes she thought she heard a car in the distance and would go wait at the edge of the camp to see if Alistair's driver could be bringing her another letter. She'd stand still and try to will the car into her vision. *Bring me a letter,* she'd repeat to herself. *Bring it now.*

Whenever she remembered him, excitement and pleasure carried her upwards as if she were moving on a tide. But she also began to feel lazy and she slept a lot. She thought she might be pregnant.

The next time Alistair stopped at the camp to deliver the mail, she took him aside to ask if he could do a test for her. "Just to make it official. I've never missed before, but maybe the change of climate has something to do with it."

"I'll need a specimen," he said. "No end of phials and retorts with me, and nothing the right size. It's always the way."

"We've got a lot of extra little cans for the paints. I'll find something."

As he was leaving, she handed him an old jam jar wrapped up in a brown paper bag. "Takes me back to my student days," he said. "Extraordinary containers I saw. Coffee jars were far and away the favorite."

"And don't say anything about it, please."

"My dear lady," he told her.

"Yes, I know. I'm only asking because it's important. And I want to be the one to break the news if there is any." She went on to ask him if she could be doing herself or a baby any harm by taking antimalaria pills. He questioned her about prescriptions and recent vaccinations. After he had driven away, she stood looking at the dust from the road as it billowed into the air. It spread out and hung in front of her for a moment like a piece of veiling across the landscape, then gradually dispersed, leaving only light and heat and the sound of a breeze in the trees nearby.

*

Stan went over his notes and copied some of the earlier jottings into his current folder. He made a recording of a long chapter on possession and the theory of substitution. He added a footnote about changelings. And he wrote a letter to Switzerland. After lunch he lay on his side with his elbow out and one hand under his cheek. He read. Across from him Millie was curled up on her cot. She looked through magazines and catalogs.

He read about lions; their power, speed and agility. It was amazing what they could do: leap over a high fence to pick up a larger, heavier animal in their jaws and then jump back over with it. Wonderful. The degree of strength in ratio to their size was certainly greater than a man's. They were also stupendously virile. Ian had told him that one of the big zoos in Europe had made a study of how often a leonine courting couple mated in a set number of minutes, and the figures were astounding. But it was the lion's character that interested

Stan; that is, the character it had been given. He had studied ballads and epic poems that likened men to all different kinds of creature – no animal was excluded from comparison. And every country or region had its own special types. But lions were universal. Most people knew what they were and every-one who was acquainted with them agreed that they were the fastest, the wildest, the most kingly, strongest, most terrifying, the proudest. And they were never afraid, never.

*

In the evening, after dinner, they played bridge. Ian kept yawning, almost as much as he had the night before, but wouldn't give up. He said that only on this safari had he learned to enjoy cards.

"Never had the time before. It's always been such an awful bore to have to entertain the clients after a hard day's work. It's grand to be able to put one's feet up, not have to go beating round the district for dirty great trophies. I often think if I were entering the profession now as a young chap, I'd only allow cameras, like everyone else. I suppose it'll come to that."

"Like Gregor Mandrake?" Millie asked.

"Who?"

"The fashion photographer. I read someplace, he was out here last year. He's famous."

"Is that the fellow's name? It doesn't surprise me. You're seriously asking if I –"

"I was joking, Ian."

"I should hope so. Frightful charlatan. Tom thought the world of him, wanted to be a cameraman for a while."

"It couldn't be real," Stan said. "It's got to be made up, a name like that."

Millie said, "You once told me everything important was made up."

"You keep resuscitating all my star quotations. I hardly remember any of them."

"Ah, that's a habit wives have," Ian said. "I've noticed that myself."

Alistair looked in on them a few days later. He'd seen Nicholas, was bringing a letter from him, and also had two scandalous stories to relate.

"Now that is kind," Pippa told him. "How should we ever know about the latest news if you didn't take pity on us? And two of them."

The first story was about the accident in the game park, which had taken place just before the death of the German nurse.

"The man who jumped out of the car," Stan said, "and the lion on the roof got him."

"That's the one. It seems now that they pushed him out. Two of the men are under arrest. They don't know what to do with the wife: charge her with complicity, or let her go. She's still a free woman, the last I heard."

"Two men," Ian repeated.

"What a feast," Pippa said appreciatively. "Were they both having an affair with the woman, or has money been changing hands? Definitely one of the best we've had."

"The other one's not so much a scandal as an outrage. More our line of country. Some poacher with his musket pointed it up in the air and fired at the London balloon – Freeman and the New Zealander, Pembroke. It's a miracle they're alive."

"Good Lord," Ian said. "He brought them down?"

"Down with a thump. Pembroke's got a broken leg, arm, and

crushed ribs. I couldn't remember his name at the time and I was in such a rush, I told matron he was called Mr. Bonebroke. She's going to be dining out on that one for years."

"Outrage is putting it mildly. I can't understand it, except out of sheer malice."

Stan said, "Maybe he thought they were looking for poachers instead of counting the game."

"What about the other one?" Pippa asked. "Freebody."

"Freeman. That's more serious. He has a fractured skull. I thought at first his neck was broken too, but it was just the way he was lying. And blood everywhere. Something they had with them was made of glass. They both looked as if they'd been shot with the pieces. Don't they make most of those expedition articles from plastic or safety glass nowadays? It was a fine old mess, I can tell you. Picking out the bits for hours."

Ian talked vehemently and at length about poachers until Stan changed the subject by saying, "I just remembered, the party we went to. The night before we left town. I was talking about that accident in the game park, and then I said something about *sub judice* and I thought everybody was going to die laughing. One of them was named Wilson, and – let me think."

After prompting from Ian and Alistair, he brought out one more name and some descriptions. Ian said, "I don't wonder they laughed. You were talking to a judge, a magistrate, and probably defending and prosecuting counsel."

Millie went to her tent to find her letters. She walked slowly in the bright light and smiled slightly. Alistair's driver was waiting for her. He gave her a folded envelope and she handed him the message she had already written. She asked, "Have you seen him?"

"No, I take the letters from my brother this time."

"I haven't seen him in a long while now."

"He was on safari, three trips."

"I know. I'm glad he's well, but I'm very impatient to see him."

The driver smiled. "Him too," he said. "He never likes to wait."

Alistair wouldn't stay for lunch. "On my rounds," he explained. Pippa suggested that if he had the time and could manage it, he should bring that other doctor – what was her name? – oh yes, Carrol, to visit them at the Whiteacres' camp. Alistair blushed. He said he'd think about it.

"Might not be a bad idea at that. She's been a bit low lately. I think she's had some sort of quarrel with Eddie."

"Over you-know-what?" Pippa asked, pointing up to the sky.

"I don't know," he said shortly. "I haven't asked."

"Well, try to bring her. We'd all like to meet her. She sounds such a nice girl."

Millie had to run after him.

"You've forgotten," she panted.

He turned, looked puzzled, then cried out, "Oh good heavens, how could I? Yes, of course. It's positive."

"Don't shout."

"I'm so sorry. Too many things to think of at once."

"She did have a quarrel about that, didn't she? She's broken up with Eddie."

"I, ah, well – I don't really –"

"I'm sure you'd be much better for her, Alistair. Just don't be a gentleman and stand aside. She'll think you don't care enough. You go right on in and propose. Down on one knee. Straightaway."

"I thought I'd better give her some time to think."

"Certainly not. If you let her think about it, you don't stand a chance."

"Really? You think not?"

"Of course not. She'll retreat into her shell for a couple of years in order to get over the Eddie business, and then she'll start looking for someone exactly like him. You just go ahead. And remember, this other thing is still my secret."

*

Ian read most of Nicholas's letter out loud. Perhaps he read all of it. Millie had an idea that some parts had been skipped at the beginning, where there was a sentence about Jill. Nicholas described the way the shooting was going, saying that he was having great difficulty in trying to make the clients stick to their licenses and not look on each day's hunt as an opportunity to outshine each other. For Pippa's benefit he listed the various excesses and comforts of the big camp, then he gave an account of the people.

As for the Whiteacres, he wrote, *I think they hate each other. Every day I go out with them, I remember that story about the wife who shoots her husband instead of the elephant. And the sleeping arrangements are in constant flux, as your friend Rollo would say. More than usual. The first thing that happened was that the engaged couple had some sort of quarrel. He moved in with Darleen; she had decided almost as soon as we put down stakes that Otis was never going to make her anything more than the secretary. To start off, she took comfort from Whiteacre. The wife, Bobsy, never said anything and they're still sharing a double tent. All this is so much worse out here than in town. When Darleen changed her allegiance to Bill, he asked his fiancée (Martha) to trade tents, as she was still in the dou-*

ble and he and Darleen were too cramped in the single. She agreed. She came to me and asked if it was understood that her ex-fiancé had paid for everything, because she was now on her own but intended to finish the safari – another one who might go off half-cocked, although maybe not. She seems much the most sensible of the lot. Showed me her engagement ring, a stone the size of my thumbnail, and said to the best of her knowledge if engagements were broken for whatever reason, the ring remained the property of the woman and she might just go round the world on her diamond to make up for the way things had turned out. She also said, "I'm still crazy about him, but I can see now it would never change. I'd have a lifetime of it." The next thing was that Bobsy Whiteacre in an extremely discreet manner made me a proposition, if that's the word. Perhaps not. I've been so bothered about Jill and the farm that I wasn't taking in much of the finer detail. A few scenes of the farce may have slipped by without my noticing. However, I pleaded ignorant and now Bert has been turned down by Martha and in revenge is after me to boot her out of the team. I hope you're following all this. And at some point Bill changed his mind and thought he'd go back to Martha, who said no. That left him still sharing the double tent with Darleen. It's been like musical chairs ever since. What we need is someone like H. Lewis to go through the place like a dose of salts – you remember what they said about the Janson show. I had a letter from him last week, says he's getting married again. Can you believe it? She has to get a divorce first. We'll see him as soon as he's done with the next set of clients. In the meantime, the extra man the Whiteacres found is supposed to be seconded to Bill and Martha. Named Bean. I've seen him about. Used to be with B & C down on the coast. On the sauce, frequently all but afloat on a tide of it. Whether his job is going to include Bobsy Whiteacre or Darleen, or even both, is anyone's guess. He doesn't *look up to it. Seems struck on Martha, but she's had enough. She plays cards with me and old Otis, who tells us about doing the tours in Norway back in the year dot, climbing over the mountains and meeting Henrik Ibsen, so he claims. A nice old boy. He says he plans to leave us soon, but has enjoyed everything immensely* AND WILL RECOMMEND US WARMLY TO EVERYONE HE KNOWS. *I'm not sleeping very well. If you can manage to join us sooner rather than later, I'd be grateful. Thank you again for everything. As ever, Nick.*

"That's it," Ian said. "Poor old Nick."

Millie said, "What was the Janson show?"

"A monumental package-holiday company that used to run booze-up tours for millionaires. All the ladies wanted to try out the tame hero, started to quarrel over him. He put it to them that, ah, he could either take them on all at once, or they could do it by rota."

"And?"

"They drew up a schedule, whose turn was when. So the story goes. He said it wasn't true. Fancy Harry getting married."

"Best thing for him," Pippa said. "Just what he needs. Everyone needs a family. I keep thinking about those poor men in the balloon, shot out of the sky like that."

"You see? I told you they weren't safe. Anything can happen."

Stan said, "What does B & C stand for? And that other one with initials?"

"Oh, it's the same one. We just call it G & T for a laugh. Referring to the sort of client they get, sort of safari they run. Sitting about in camp, drinking gin and tonic."

"And not always such a bad idea," Pippa said.

*

Stan had a dream. He dreamt that he was in a jungle at night. The thick-growing trees were slung with creepers and looked like the background to the Tarzan movies of his youth, but he knew that they were in the East and that he was in the war. Other men, soldiers, were crowding up in back of him. They were all in the army together. A man came out from behind a trunk just ahead: his brother, Sandy, who said, "Where were you? I've been waiting for you." His brother was dark, like an African. Stan thought that he had changed into a Negro, then he realized that it was just camouflage blacking. There were fires and detonations in front of them. Whenever one of the explosions came, the glare lit up the night trees so you could see they were actually green. People kept moving forward on their bellies all around him. Suddenly there was a stillness. Then Sandy brought his hand chopping down hard on the back of Stan's neck. He said, "It's your turn now." There was a white burst of light that covered everything. Stan felt his head snatched back into the night. His body jumped together. He was wiped away, he died. And then he was awake, his chest fluttering as if his heart were spilling out over it, and warmth falling away from him in rivulets like the seawater off a rock.

Millie too had a dream, at the time when the deepest part of the darkness was about to thin out and lift. She dreamt that she was being married. She was standing next to Henry, holding his hand. She had on a long white dress and the necklace he had given her. All around them their wedding guests were dancing in a circle. The people went so fast that they melted into each other, blending like paints that ran together. Henry said, "From the first moment I saw you." She died for joy.

Early in the morning they were climbing over each other in the small tent to find their clothes and Millie said, "You've stepped on my alligator. And I can't find the boa constrictor."

"Wait till I'm awake, will you?"

"Paintings, Stan. Move your foot."

"I don't know what you think you're proving, Millie. I'm having wet dreams now. This is ridiculous."

"I don't see why. For years you don't want me for anything but the shopping and the cooking. Now I want a divorce and suddenly you want bed. That's the ridiculous part."

"You don't really, do you? You want a divorce?"

"Yes, Stan. I do. Pick up your foot, please."

"Oh, the hell with that. Look, we'll talk about it."

"Whenever you like."

"We'll talk about it later."

Millie smiled. She said, "Sure. Just remember, when you've left it too late, I've already done my talking."

"I mean, we'll really talk about it."

"Fine." She pushed the flap aside and moved out of the tent. He went after her, holding his shirt in his hand. He said, "You don't really want a divorce, or you wouldn't be here."

"I'm waiting for something."

Stan looked around him at the empty plains, the blank, hot sky. "Here?" he asked.

"I'm waiting for the right time. And for you to accept it."

"Sure," he said. "That's great. That's just great." He put on his shirt and started to do up the buttons. He thought of a really good argument against everything she had said, but when he looked up to tell her, saw that she had already walked away from him.

*

Millie and Pippa traveled a long way from camp that day in search of good views. They settled near a majestic slanted tree that rose from a small eminence above a grassfield. The field was of many colors, from pale almost-white, to a deep russet-gold. Pippa set up her easel while Millie stared ahead.

You're with me all the time, she thought. *I keep remembering everything. I tingle all over. I can't wait.*

The moment she came into the room, he stood up from the bed, where he'd been sitting. He said, "I forgot to give you this." He took something from his pocket and held it out. In the palm of his hand was a gold chain. He lifted it up.

She said, "It's beautiful."

"And you're beautiful," he said.

"But I can't. How would I explain it? What could I tell my husband?"

"Tell him you bought it," he said. "If you really get stuck, tell him you found it in the street. That's what I always used to say. Nobody believed me, either."

Pippa came and stood beside Millie. She asked, "How is it?"

"I've been dreaming. It's so nice here. But I just wondered: the best view is probably from out there, looking back. Looking at the tree. Don't you think?"

"That's for another day. It's a much more difficult proposition. The light."

Millie walked over and looked at the beginning Pippa had made. The painting evidently aimed for an impression of the field's different colors, their several ways of holding and shedding light. At the moment, it looked like a picture of a hairy rug.

"A series of washes afterwards," Pippa said.

"Mm."

They ate their sandwiches and drank cold tea out of thermos flasks. Robert wandered over to the other side of the field for a while, to join two men he gossiped with and who usually shared his meals outside camp.

They dozed when the sun was at its height. Later, when Pippa went back to her landscape, Millie decided to start another painting. As she progressed, she was filled with the idea and worked very fast, making a picture that showed an African poacher shooting down the green-and-white checked London balloon. But she was disappointed at the result. The incident had been a serious business and she had made it seem comic. Her rendition was like a cartoon. She thought she'd tear it up.

"Any luck?" Pippa called. Her sketch, with the added washes, now indicated the softness and bushy growth of the field.

"That's nice," Millie said.

"Something's wrong, though."

"Not that I can see. Something to do with the way the shadows are falling? I never notice things like that."

"Of course, it's the shadows. I should have asked you sooner. Here. And here."

When Millie turned to walk back to her improvised easel, she saw that Robert and his friends were crowded around it and obviously talking about the scene she had brought to life.

"I just thought of something," she said. "I painted a picture of the poacher, and you can't see his face, but maybe everyone will think the real man is dressed that way and has that kind of a gun and so on."

"What's this?"

"Come take a look."

"May I see, please?" Pippa said to Robert. The group stood back. Pippa's face became contorted.

"That's the trouble," Millie said. "I think I'd better tear it up right now."

"No, my dear. Certainly not. It's priceless."

"Can you explain that I don't know what the man really looks like?"

"I see. Yes, that's a bit tricky. It's understood that you weren't there at the time, but if not, then you must have dreamt it, and dreams reveal the truth."

"Especially since the balloon is exactly the way it should be. Can you just say I could paint him out and put in a different man? I'm no good at the complicated stuff, long sentences and everything."

"I'm afraid you've now established the magical vision of this painted man being the one who did the deed."

"Lucky I didn't give him a special hat or shirt. I still don't understand it. Everybody here sees photographs and other pictures, even movies and TV. And those self-service snapshot booths in town. Even the Masai were using them. All the time."

"The Photo-Me kiosks. Of course. But this is the old guard, you know. Not the modern generation. Not like Tom."

"It's dry already," Millie said. "I guess it's a classic of its time now. Too late to do anything about it."

They started back long before Stan and Ian, who had spent their morning tracking a wounded lioness. The only time she broke cover, they could see that there was an arrow or dart, or spearpoint of some kind still lodged down behind her shoulder. She led them across a dry gully and up into a formation of craggy rocks. Ian threw his hat on the ground and stamped.

"There's no way of getting her out of there. No way at all."

"Smart cookie."

"Absolutely. I don't know why so often the ones that deserve to survive are just the ones that don't."

"It happens to people too, haven't you noticed? It's practically axiomatic."

"True enough."

"And in the end, it's only a reprieve, anyway. Nobody survives for very long."

"Rotten feeling to leave a wounded beast. Put her out of her misery before the hyenas get at her."

"She might take a few with her."

"Still, there it is. Let's go."

They shot eland for the evening meal on the way back to camp and traveled through country that was mellow and glowing from a sun about to set. As he turned his face against the yellow and rosy blur cast over the land, Stan thought it was a little like the beginning stages of inebriation. And then, as he was looking into the fields, a memory came to him – as suddenly and vividly as a shiver running over his skin – of Jack's flat in London: the four of them intertwined under just such a soft, drunken light in a tangle of limbs, and of himself doing things, having things done to him and not being sure who was doing them, and not caring.

He had two dreams that night. The first was like an echo of his afternoon vision: he was naked, pressed deep within a coiled and slithering knot of other naked bodies. But all at once it wasn't London any more. One of the women was Millie. And the man, when they were at last face to face, was his brother, Sandy.

His second dream began as one of those nightmares where

you believe you are awake. He was out hunting with Ian and they picked up the track of the lioness they had been following. This time it led across a pretty landscape filled with trees. Soon they came to scattered buildings and the beginnings of towns, but still the trail led on. It began to look like home. He recognized a neighbor's house from a few streets away. And then they saw a clearing full of Africans in masks and carrying shields and spears; they were chanting and dancing around in a circle. Ian pushed him. "They're waiting for you," he said. Stan didn't want to enter the circle. He knew that if he did, he would die. "It's a trial of manhood," Ian said. "It's a fertility rite." He shoved Stan hard, into the middle of the circle, and the same thing happened that had happened to him the night before: slamming him in the base of the neck, grabbing his head away backwards into nothingness and the white snowfield blinding across his eyes.

He woke again and stayed awake for a long time. He said to himself that things couldn't go on like this.

My brother, he thought. *Father named him Alexander. A bronze star name. But Sandy wasn't any braver than I am. He used to cover up his eyes in the movies. He was afraid of the moths divebombing in the bathroom. They were never proud of me that way. And he wasn't worth it, anyhow. I know that. It's because he did the heroic thing and died. But I don't have to prove anything. I am not a coward.*

They moved for the last time, to join the group at the big camp. On the night before, they toasted each other as though they would never meet again, since from that time onward, Ian would be occupied with the Whiteacres and their many guests.

Their route carried them at one point through true farming country and they saw a great many people and villages, which they had avoided so far in their moves from place to place. Millie was interested. Stan, on the other hand, was offended by this sudden evidence of domesticated civilization in a country he had become used to thinking of as a hunter's Garden of Eden. The villages contained bicycles, beer parlors, sewing machines, women wearing tailored dresses and men with suits. Scrawny cattle, tended by children, roamed across the outskirts. There were more young people than in the villages he had seen so far; he had been introduced to very traditional, outmoded places, where the sons grew up wanting to get out fast and go to work for the safari companies or for the government, and the daughters had dreams of living a modern life in the big cities.

The road was used by many groups traveling on foot. An old man, who held a flowered parasol, was one of the few pedestrians to whom Tom gave a lift. There seemed to be an established etiquette about picking passengers up on the road: you didn't take everyone who asked, otherwise it became like a game. And no very young children, who only wanted rides for fun and then called out to large numbers of their friends to come join in.

Whether near villages or out on the plains, dust rose around them as they moved forward. Some places were worse than others; often a turn in the road would bring them out into a new stretch of country that almost seemed to be part of a different climate.

They arrived early in the afternoon, expecting to find a camp stocked with all the people mentioned in the letters they had received, but met only Nicholas himself and the cook-house crew and gunbearers.

Nicholas helped with the unpacking. He said, "You wouldn't believe the explanations. You couldn't. I shan't even try."

"Joshua knows," Tom said.

"Never mind, then. I'll tell it." He said that only two days before, Alistair's friend Carrol, after a final quarrel with Eddie, had driven into town in search of a lawyer. Eddie had gone back to the balloon just in time to be able to hitch a ride with Bernhard's girlfriend, Karen, while Bernhard himself drove Otis and Martha to town. They had been followed by Darleen, who wanted to return to her duties as Otis's secretary, and Bob, who had again decided he needed Martha back.

Stan said, "So now it's musical cars instead of musical chairs. It must feel like the place is empty."

"It feels bloody marvelous. And there's an even chance it may stay like this for a bit."

The Whiteacres, together with friends of theirs named Stone, had gone off to the coast for several weeks. They had fired Jonathan Bean before leaving.

"Saves me the bother," Ian said.

"That was the last straw, Bean. I couldn't even put it in a letter. Talk – you should have heard him talk. Made me want to wash the camp with carbolic from top to bottom. That whining voice, and he's delighted. 'Oh, I hear you're having troubles at home, isn't that a pity!' I thought of shooting him. God's truth. Making it look like an accident. Had to keep myself on a tight rein every minute of the day. There was a great temptation to follow precedent and just stay pissed. It's been sheer bloody hell."

The country they were in contained all kinds of animals and so many different terrains that it was as if their camp had been the crossroads for a geological revolution. They had desert, forest, plains, hills and one spot full of streams, trees and meadows.

Stan now spent most of his time hunting with Nicholas, while Ian went out early with Tom. For the first two days they barely spoke. The next morning, Stan said, "Tell me about the game," and Nicholas talked, with many pauses so long that they became silences. Stan let him take his time and kept himself from interrupting with too many questions. They ate their lunch in the shade of some trees and rested. Stan nearly went to sleep. He asked about rituals, any ceremonies connected with lion.

"Oh, Harry is the expert on lion," Nicholas said. "But there are those initiations. It's all a bit of a nuisance now. You know, the Whiteacres were expecting to have every kind of show put on for them. They wanted to go to villages the way one would go out to the theater. Drove me mad."

"I guess you can let Ian handle that side of it from now on. He'll take care of all those things when they come back."

"Ian is marvelous with clients. But he sometimes has a filthy temper."

"Well, like he says: they've paid."

Stan leaned back and pulled the brim of his hat down. The world around him grew hotter and whiter, until it seemed to approach incandescence. Everything became silent. And nothing moved; there wasn't even any dust in the air. He slept lightly for a quarter of an hour. When he woke, Nicholas was sitting just as he had been, staring out into the landscape as though into the future. Maybe he wasn't seeing what he was looking at.

Maybe he was wondering whether his wife had considered him incapable of making a success of their lives. The farm wasn't bringing in any money, nor was the business doing as well as it should be. That was all right for Ian, who had saved something and had three grown children earning their living, and who was the type who didn't really give a damn anyway. Nicholas was more like a country boy from back home; slow, sincere, meeting his worries like a man twice his age.

"Do you know the people in the balloon?" Stan asked. "The Scandinavians?"

"Of course."

"Do they ever take passengers?"

"Yes. I've been up with them. It's a bit cramped, but they've got everything. Full of modern comforts, failsafe devices, unsmashable whatnots. Not like poor old Pembroke. Interesting to see the place from above."

"What do they look like?"

"What do what look like?"

"Bernhard and the girlfriend. I actually dreamt about going up in the balloon with them."

"He's my size, more or less. Brown hair, gray eyes. Short beard like the Kon Tiki mask. She's small, fair, slanted eyes, blue. Looks rather like a blonde eskimo, very wild."

"Weird?"

"No, wild."

"I was thinking about the rumor going around, about all of them up there together. Maybe you haven't heard it."

"Oh yes, I've heard."

"Think it's true?"

"If it's not, it should be."

"Oh?"

"Why not? Makes a good story."

"I meant really."

"Who knows?"

"They aren't the same. In my dream, they looked different."

"Makes sense. Dreams are always different. That's what the word means: something real in another form, everything falsified."

Stan started to say it had been the one good dream he had had in the past few weeks, but he stopped. "Do you ever have bad dreams?" he asked.

"Not any more. I did for a while. Frightful. About the children being killed. About Jill. Then I stopped having any at all."

On their way back to camp they took a different route. The road ran along a stand of trees and the slanting sun threw slats of light and dark across their path. It reminded Stan of something. He thought about London again, about Jack, about Nicholas. And about his brother. People forgive you so much if you're killed in a war. It's the brave ones who die, everyone knows that. Your photograph goes up on the piano or on the mantelpiece, your medals in the drawer. They especially forgive you for not fulfilling the promise they saw in you. It's their promise in any case, not yours. And you are spared the failure they put upon you for not becoming their second self.

For years he had felt angry with himself, and he'd taken it out on Millie. Not till London did he begin to put the blame on his parents and his brother; there was nothing wrong with him – there never had been. It was them, and the way they had treated him. And he had to be free of them, if only it wasn't too late.

As they came across the fields, already growing dark, he was again aware of the sense of dread – the suffocating, deathly feeling he couldn't explain, and which had first fallen across him as he'd stood on the sidewalk with Millie back in town. He was afraid that he might really lose her. He had never seriously thought it before. It was inconceivable. That she should want a divorce – that he could understand. But naturally it would never happen, because it would only be a wish. And yet, nothing was the same now. She herself was like a self-assured and charming woman he'd just been introduced to and whose thoughts he could not guess at. He would have to be as careful about winning back her attention, and approach her with as much guile and tenderness, as if she were a deer in the forest.

And he would have to go slow. He wanted to say something that night but when they entered the tent, he didn't know how to begin. He decided to wait.

He lay in the dark with his eyes open. He thought about Myra. The red jacket she had, the afternoon when his watch stopped, and that day in the early spring when he saw her after squash and she hooked her fingers into the collar of his sweater and asked, "Did little wifie knit you this? Is she sitting at home making doilies?" "Don't talk like that," he'd told her, but the truth was that Millie was so dejected and woebegone at the time, such a sad sack that he stayed away from the apartment as much as possible. He was conscious of her ridiculousness even when he could see that she should be pitied. And he had long ago talked himself into condoning his infidelities, even before the question of having children – or not having them – had become such a large, concealed part of their lives. It often seemed to him that by being with another woman he was getting even with Millie for her dreariness. He deserved something better, after all. So, he had not once thought he should feel guilty, not even later about her friend, Sally Murchison – and that really would have been a mess if it had come out. The Murchisons, both of them – Jerry, too – were friends who had known them from the beginning, when Stan had first started at the college. Jerry had been his colleague. He felt badly about it all at once. But at the time, and for a long while, nothing. Only now. Now it was unbelievable to him that he should have acted in such a way. And he was ashamed.

Biologists talk about the aggressive instincts of animals, he thought, *but people themselves take the cake every time. They won't let a thing alone even after the victims are dead. They stand out among the earth's population as members of the one species whose hatreds and fears are mostly directed against itself. You'd think they would have died out a long time ago.*

*

Nicholas sat over morning tea with Millie and Pippa. The women praised the opulent comforts of the Whiteacres' camp, especially the showers. They had both washed their hair earlier in the morning.

"It's sad to have to admit that it should make such a difference," Pippa said, "but it does."

"And for me, it's shaving," Nicholas said. "I'm quite content to go about unwashed for weeks, but if I can't shave, I begin to feel scruffy."

"You've never wanted to grow a beard like Ian?" Millie asked.

"Never. Only if I developed one of those skin complaints, or a case of sunblisters."

He said there was nothing like tea, then he asked to see some of the works of art. He expressed particular interest in the picture of the balloon and its assassin. Millie said again that she wished she had never had the idea, but he was delighted with the painting.

"They're like children's drawings, I know," she said.

"No, they're not. They're more like what-do-you-call-it."

"Primitive art," Pippa said. "Folk art. They're childlike, but never crude or inept. Naïve, that's the one."

"Oh boy. Just like the magazines. And here we have an example of an early attempt." Millie held out a picture of a zebra. It had an expression on its face like a mule, or perhaps a camel. Nicholas laughed. He kept looking back at the picture and smiling. Millie presented it to him. She said, "That's what they're for. When you stop enjoying it, take it off the wall and put something else there."

*

In the afternoon she and Pippa painted, as usual. Pippa quickly became dedicated to a configuration of branches in the near distance and hardly looked up from her work except to check with the landscape.

Millie doodled for a while, then got up to stretch. As she raised her arms above her head, she suddenly thought that something was about to happen. She pulled her hands back. She felt so dizzy that she almost fell. Everything was silent and she was frightened.

She turned around once. Nothing had changed. She turned around twice. Robert and Odinga were standing where they had been before, and Odinga's cousin, Ajuma, was playing a game with two sticks and some stones on the ground. It was all the same as when she had risen to her feet, but something wasn't right.

On the way to their tent that evening, Stan shook his shoulders and stood still. Millie asked, "Something wrong?"

"I don't know. I just got the creeps all of a sudden."

"Me, too. Something someone said today or something I saw, I don't know – gave me the most horrible feeling. I guess it sort of built up. One minute it wasn't there, and then it was."

"I felt pretty bad yesterday, too," he said. "I suddenly got really scared that you might leave me. I couldn't stand it, Millie."

"I think you could. When you get used to the idea. It's just the shock, that's all. At the moment, you're used to me being around."

"That's a lousy thing to say."

"Oh, Stan. All the lousy things to say I've saved up for so many years, and now it's too late. I'm not even trying. If I say anything, it's just what I think, that's all. I'm not trying to hurt you. I don't even want to any more."

"You mean, you did?"

"Of course," she said, standing at the entrance of the tent. "Pay you back. It's natural. You did a real all-out demolition job on me. It succeeded because I loved you. And then when you quit, I started doing your work for you. I was dead on my feet for years. I didn't wake up till London."

She went into the tent, leaving him standing outside and wondering stupidly if her days in London could have been just like his; could she have picked up some people and every night, while he was with the others – was it so crazy? He stepped into the tent.

"How did London wake you up?"

"Well, I've been talking my head off about it to anyone who'd listen. *Romeo and Juliet.* Covent Garden. Etcetera."

"Oh, that," he said.

"It changed my life. I should have seen it years ago."

He laughed. He knew it was some kind of game. She was so calm. Playing hide-and-seek, of course. At last she'd learned how. She was teaching him a lesson. That was all right. He'd say, "Yes, I know" and "Forgive me" and eventually she would forgive, as long as he'd been through this period of repenting. It had to be that way, because now everything was falling into place and he realized that what he wanted was the chance to find the happiness he could have had many years ago, if he'd recognized it. And it could only come through Millie.

*

Over drinks the next evening, Nicholas joined the Fosters in encouraging Millie to take up the business of painting as a profession. She smiled and said she'd think it over; it wasn't such a bad idea.

When they were alone together, Stan said, "We are still married, you know."

"But not for much longer."

"Look, Millie, you've made your point. I haven't been trying as much as I could have."

"Oh, Stan. Now, listen. We've both changed a lot. We still know each other pretty well, but in a way we don't. We don't have anything to draw on any more. I don't believe you care about me. It's as simple as that. I don't really believe you ever did. I thought so at the time, and I'll give you the benefit of the doubt and say I think you did, too, but that's all over."

"Are you crazy? I love you, Millie. Are you saying you don't love me any more, not at all?"

"I'm still very fond of you, Stan."

"Fond of me. Oh, great. Shove that."

"Very fond of you, despite the fact that you can annoy me more than almost any other person I've ever met. It hasn't helped that everything I tried to do, you took special pains to tear down. Something was wrong with the way we organized our family right from the start. I know you have this thing about: if only we'd had children, but believe me, that would've made it twice as bad for me. Everybody thinks Jill is in a mess – at least Nicholas is on her side. What I'm trying to say is that for some reason, it made you feel good every time I failed at something – especially when I failed to please you. That meant you were free to go your own way, right? So, we've had too many years of that. And now it's all different, and I've come back to being human again. It's because other people are there around me and you haven't had the chance to keep tearing me down. Now, I don't care how we work this. I can go back to town tomorrow morning, or I can move into a different tent, or we can go on like this, but at the end of this trip, we say goodbye."

"All those years, you thought I was trying to make you feel unsure of yourself? Tearing you down?"

"And you succeeded. I wasn't all that sure of myself, anyway."

"Your father once told me you –"

"Oh, what does my father know about anything? He doesn't even like women – he only likes his comfort. As long as he's all right, everything is all right. He's the baby in the family: he comes first. And she resents it, and we noticed very early on how much she dislikes her life. I used to think, if only I'd gotten out sooner. But now it's better, and I'm stronger for it."

A stream of talk came out of her. He felt frustrated and maddened. He grabbed hold of her and shook her. She hit him and jabbed him with her knee. He was ready to tear her apart. She said, "If you do, I swear I'll shoot you. Jesus, all the years I've been sweet and kind to you through every damn humiliation you put on me, and this is all you think of me, you bastard."

He let go immediately, as if he'd been burned. He had never heard her use such words. He was shocked, more than he could have imagined, to hear her using them to his face, calling him names. He collapsed on to his camp bed, panting. She too was gasping. He had made her cry, but not with sorrow as she used to; with anger and desperation.

He said, "I'm so lonesome."

"We're in a beautiful country, on a luxury safari, surrounded by hot-and-cold running servants and gross plenty, and you're on the track of your religious theory. There isn't any reason to be lonesome. Write a letter to your friend Myra. Or Sally Murchison. Or that Belgian girl who worked in the library, and all the others, even in London. I'm not lonesome. I'll talk to Ian in the morning about getting a separate tent."

"Don't do that. It'll be all right."

"I don't see why I should have to put up with this."

"Leave it. Better me than somebody else. You move out, and I bet Nicholas would be under the netting before you knew what hit you."

"Incredible," she said. "God, this is incredible. Good night, Stan."

She seemed to go to sleep straightaway, confident that he wouldn't try to disturb her a second time.

*

He couldn't sleep for a long while. He kept going over what she had said, and remembering the tone of her voice: it had been level and controlled – dispassionate, as though she were beyond him, standing far away from him and feeling contempt. And now he couldn't even get through to her in the simplest way. He couldn't touch her. If they had had children – but maybe she was right about that, too. All he knew for certain was that she must not leave. They had to stay together, no matter what. She had really been prepared to shoot him. Well, he was prepared too, if she tried to leave. He wouldn't be able to stand it. He couldn't imagine himself left alone while she went on leading a different existence somewhere else. They belonged together.

He couldn't sleep for so long that he finally got up and put his head through the tent flap and then stood just outside the entrance, his jacket over his shoulders. It was cold. He looked up at the stars, not precisely the stars of his childhood, but pretty good. Always good; one of the things in life that was never a disappointment. It was always good to look at the stars.

He listened to the sounds of the night. The voices of the animals called to each other for food, love, battle. It was as noisy as standing near a highway. He didn't know how to interpret everything he heard, but he was sure that it included the false threat of the meek as well as the real warning of the killer.

All of them were out there, acting. And pulling tricks on each other, attacking and eating, the weak going down to the strong and the few to the multitude. It was the way they stayed alive. All the many disguises they had: they made themselves sound different, and they could make themselves look different, too – change color and size, where a man would need the aid of clothing, makeup, added or removed hair. Even the cat his parents had had at home had been able to transform itself in an instant. They'd found her at the edge of the yard one day, holding her ground against an intruding gang of bigger, rougher-looking cats; she'd been a small, slim and vivacious animal with an affectionate disposition, but when Stan reached her she had swollen up until she was almost round as a ball, and the baleful howls that continued to break from her altered body had made him want to put her down again fast.

When an animal changed, there was reason for the change. But what was the reason in people deceiving each other? One of the midwestern universities had done research on the subject recently and proven that man had an inborn capacity for deception. The doctors there had studied children and found that from the very earliest years it was characteristic of humankind to justify itself: if you asked children something, they would hand you an explanation – anything, no matter how nonsensical it was.

That was people being false to each other. And why, as if that weren't strange enough, did they mislead themselves? They pretended to be different from what they were. They didn't actually change, because the only real change came from within, but they told themselves that they had. They lied.

He too had been pretending. All his life he had been pretending not to feel fear. And he'd always been afraid. That was what made people cruel – fear. Only now was it beginning to release him, but he thought perhaps he was losing something else with it as it let go.

He went back inside and lay down. At some point just before the turn of the night and gradual lightening of the sky towards the pre-dawn, he began to fall asleep. And as he did, he heard someone out in the camp clear his throat and cough. He listened, expecting it to happen again. The sound had left him with an impression of suspense. Someone was out there, keeping watch. But whoever it was didn't give a second sign and Stan fell asleep waiting for it.

*

Millie was up before the rest of the camp. She washed, dressed and slipped away from the tent, out into the morning. She smelled food. The calling and answering of voices in the cook-house came to her as a vague murmur from the far side of the camp. Then, closer, she heard someone cough.

She walked a couple of steps forward. In front of her, a few yards away, a shape moved against the background and stopped.

It was a lion. Right in the middle of the camp and looking straight at her. It wasn't a young or immature one – it was what everyone had in mind by the phrase "The King of the Jungle": a magnificent animal in its prime, large and with an enormous shaggy head framed by a superb mane.

Behind her she heard a tiny click and Nicholas saying softly, "Don't make a sudden movement. Back off very, very slowly and to your right. That's good. A bit more."

She moved to her right again in a slow-motion stretching walk.

"Just a bit more," Nicholas whispered, but at that moment the lion turned quickly and rushed away. Millie too turned and ran, bumping into Nicholas, who put his arm around her. He kissed her on the cheek.

"Extraordinary," he said. "I thought he was coming on, and then he just pushed off like that, had a change of heart." He kept his arm around her waist.

She said, "It was like something out of a dream. I didn't know lions ever grew that big."

"Not often, no. That was a splendid specimen. First-rate. Perhaps the best I've seen." He took his hand from her waist, placed it on her shoulder and walked towards the cookhouse tent with her.

"I thought it was a person," she said. "I heard somebody cough."

"That was the lion. It's one of the sounds they make. It's not always the growling one hears at the beginning of the pictures, or the roaring."

They drank tea in the small tent. She asked him about growing up in Africa, about school, friends, family.

"I've never been one to brood over past history," he said, "but now there are memories that keep coming back to me. I don't know why they should. They seem to have no connection with anything. I can't understand it."

"It's because you're worried. You're worried about your family."

"I suppose that's it. It's good of you to listen."

"It's good of you to talk to me." She put her hand on top of his.

Pippa called from outside. She lifted the entry flap and joined them. The others didn't wake for nearly an hour.

Stan was the last up. He had woken feeling lightheaded and taking in everything at a distance. When he saw Millie walking past the painting tent, he said, "Did you hear? Somebody shot a lion here in the camp."

"No, it was Nicholas, and the lion suddenly just turned around and ran away. He was coming straight at me."

"You? Tell me from the beginning."

He kept looking at her as she talked. She looked all right. It was hard to believe she might have been hurt. All at once it was hard for him to believe anything. He felt drugged.

Breakfast helped a little. And afterwards he went to talk to Ian. He found him checking the rifles.

"I thought we were going to that village."

Ian turned, said, "Oh," and looked exasperated. Something had gone wrong with the plans. Or maybe he'd just forgotten. "I told Amos I'd help him with something, go shooting later. Nick can take you."

"Millie might want to come too, just for once."

"Oh?"

"We almost never see each other in the daytime any more."

"Your work may not get any forrader if the people you interview decide to keep mum. You know what it's going to be like. They expect one guest, male, and one interpreter, ditto, who has the right references. No tourists, no women."

"Sure. The real authentic stuff."

"Not in English, perhaps uncomfortable, and both of you will undoubtedly be forced to sit through hours of speeches, not to mention what you'll have to eat and drink for the sake of courtesy."

"Fermented milk and stuff like that?"

"And the odd eyeball floating in muck. I've known it happen."

"I'll see you later," Stan said. As soon as he saw Nicholas, he asked about the eating and drinking.

"No, no. I'll see to that. He's in a foul mood today. We'll be all right. The usual drill. But it's a fair distance. It's going to be a long day. We should have started earlier."

"Was that you out walking around so early, when it was still dark?"

"Yes. I couldn't sleep."

"I heard you coughing."

"That wasn't me," he said. "That was the lion."

*

The two women stayed in camp. Pippa had a headache – or perhaps, she said, just possibly a hangover – and thought she might rest till the afternoon. She had also had for the past two days a persistent feeling that there was something in her eye; an eyelash might have worked its way down under the lower lid, to keep touching the eyeball as she blinked. Ian had tried to find it, but hadn't been much help and was then hurt at her abrupt dismissal of him. She was lying down in her tent when a landrover drove up and came to a halt in the clearing they had named "the car park."

Millie heard the sound of arrival. She thought it might be Alistair and she walked around the back of the camp to meet him, but saw Rupert Hatchard coming towards her. She hurried to him, smiling.

He didn't smile. As he came nearer, she realized that something serious had come up and that it must be pretty bad. She stopped in front of him.

"I'm glad I found you alone," he said. "I have bad news."

"I know. I can see."

"He's dead. He told me if anything ever went wrong, I was to come to you and tell you the truth. He has enemies. People are always telling lies about him. It was Hart and McBride who did it."

She moved her mouth, to ask what had happened. Her throat had almost closed. She put her hands out, as if to protect herself.

"He tried to keep the poachers away from his territory.

They knew they couldn't do anything in his country, so they set out to nobble him. They wouldn't even do it themselves. They paid other men to do it for them. That means they'll be caught in the end, of course, but that's small comfort."

"No," Millie said.

"He trusted me with – because I said how much I liked you."

"Yes, I see. I'm glad. I'm glad I heard it from you, but I can't think. I don't want it to be true."

"I brought your letters. I thought you'd want me to."

"Of course. That was thoughtful. That was kind." Her voice faded away. She closed her eyes.

"He was so good to Isabel," he said. "And me, naturally. He gave me no end of gen for the books. In fact, he was the one who made me believe I could do it. He could make you believe in yourself."

"Oh, yes. More than anybody I ever met, made you love the world. So much fun. I can't stand it. To be happy, finally. Did they hurt him? Say they didn't. Say it was quick."

She was in tears, snorting, spluttering, holding her head in her hands. He led her over to the landrover. A second man – an additional driver, or perhaps just a friend – who had been leaning against the fender, moved away. Rupert made her sit down inside.

While she cried, he told her that the four hired men had tried to make it look like any other drunken fight in a bar, but there were witnesses. And they would talk. Harry was greatly loved by many people, and also greatly feared. There were those who would testify to the truth because they were superstitiously convinced of the power he might have to avenge himself on them, even after death, if they didn't. At least a dozen bystanders knew the men's names. Six who were willing to speak had actually seen three of the four pinion him while the fourth cut his throat.

"I don't believe they'll live to be brought to book," Rupert said. "And I wouldn't want to be in the shoes of Marcus Hart or Pat McBride. Every man, woman and child in Harry's territory will be out for blood, you'll see."

Millie wailed, "I loved him so much. I don't know what to do. I feel like I've died. I hate everything."

He patted her on the back, smoothed her hair, put the small bundle of letters into her lap.

"It must have been instantaneous," he said. "And he was fighting hard – that would have lessened any pain. He loved you too. He kept saying: when Millie and I do this, when Millie and I do that. I can't really believe it either, even now. I'm not a man who has many friends. I never had the knack of making friends. And now he's gone."

"We prepared," Nicholas translated, "for the feast, for the bride who would come. All the village ... um ... Hang on. Right. This isn't the central village, but it's near." He asked a question, was drawn into a conversation, and spoke at some length. The answer was even longer.

Stan shifted his gaze from the man sitting opposite them to the brown roofs of the huts beyond. Everything outside the canopied shade where they sat appeared vibrant with light, effervescent, almost ready to burst into flame. He could hear children's voices coming from a place far beyond any point to which his line of vision reached.

Nicholas said, "They all prepared for the big feast and the

god was supposed to put in an appearance with the bride, but now they're going to celebrate it in a different way because he's returned to his people – this is where it's confusing, because they talk about themselves as his people, too. But I think the idea is that he's gone back to the lion."

"That's great. That's the kind of thing I need."

"And he's going to take the bride with him. She's human."

"Are these ceremonies going to involve human sacrifice?"

"I hadn't thought of that."

"It sounds right. Ask him."

"Certainly not. I wouldn't want to offend him by mentioning it. And if it were true, there'd be no hope of getting a straight answer."

"You think they might tether a girl out in the open at night and let the lions come for her?"

"I suppose that's why they made you a professor, for dreaming up ideas like that."

Nicholas spoke to the tribesman again. And all at once, Stan wondered if everything he and Nicholas had just said to each other had been understood. When the man answered and his words were again translated, Stan felt angry at himself for not having waited until afterwards to talk freely.

"There's going to be food, drink, a lot of dances, and singing. They're going to tell the story of the god. They'll make a doll, dress it up, have a parade, enormous, to the sacred place, and leave the statue of the bride for the god to come for it. All the villages in the district are going to take part. No outsiders. That means us."

"Oh, but surely if we –"

"No. Not even outsiders who are near neighbors. No one who doesn't come from this part of the country. They believe it, you see. It's their religion. I've never heard of it. And there's a lot that he says it wouldn't be right to talk about."

"Ask what the god was like when he was in his human form."

Through Nicholas, the man said, "The old men loved him, the women loved him, the children loved him, the young people; everyone loved him. He made us happy. He made us laugh. He made us rich."

"Rich?" Stan said. "How?"

The tribesman looked shaken for a moment. Then, when Nicholas asked, he pointed to his heart.

Contrary to Stan's expectations, they hadn't had to eat or drink anything, or watch any show. They had been escorted to a deserted corner of the village and now, as they left, could hear the small, high voices singing a lively song, but still could not see anyone. The children were in another part of the place. He was about to ask if they could look around, or see the singers, but Nicholas sent him a swift, cautioning wink and made a lengthy thank-you speech. Judging by something in the tone of his voice, Stan assumed it to be extremely ornate. He added his own short thanks in English and had his words translated, although he was sure by now that it wasn't necessary.

As they drove away, Nicholas said, "Something isn't right."

Stan started to talk about Jack's theory that the whole business was just a cover for an ordinary protection racket.

"I was thinking of something else," Nicholas said. "There's been a bloody great epidemic of poaching in the past few years. Ivory. That means riches, even shared out among a few villages. But the place they kept telling me was the center of the ceremony – I know it. That's Harry Lewis's district. Not great elephant country. Still – if the business went on somewhere else,

but the songs about the leader started up in another place . . .
no, that's no good. I don't suppose it could be that they're all
just songs like any others and people sing them for pleasure?
And then they begin to compete against each other, to see who
can make the best song? I must say, they don't look wonderfully
prosperous here. Not unusually so."

"Is this guy Lewis connected with poaching?"

"On the contrary. But he'd know about anything that went
on there. It's the village he recruits most of his men from.
They practically worship him there."

"Oh," Stan called out suddenly. He had caught sight of a
striped balloon up in the sky. "There's the lovenest," he said.
"Purple and black, very nice." In his dream, the balloon had
been red.

"It's a dark blue, in fact. Mauve and blue."

"It looks like it's going pretty fast."

"Hard to tell. The light can be deceptive. As you know."

"That land over there, where it's headed. And back beyond
the rise there for forty miles or so – what else can you tell me
about it?"

"Like what?"

"People, game."

"Six – I think about six – villages. And a lot of lion."

"More than in other areas?"

"Much more. It's like a game park. I think the people there
must have a closed season on them at certain times of the year.
Antelope, zebra, and so on, but those are in a normal ratio to
other areas. The lion there are in a very concentrated high
number."

"A local system of open and closed hunting would be
enough to account for it?"

"And if they keep people out. It would have to be agreed. I don't know anything for certain in any case. Only a guess."

"Have you ever come across anything you could call lion worship here – a religious cult of some kind?"

"No. Why? You don't think this is the spot marked X, do you?"

Stan's face was still directed up into the air but he said, "Well, it's beginning to look like it."

*

"Be a dear and look at my eye, would you?" Pippa asked. Rupert leaned over her face. Millie looked out at the bright ground, the hot sky. She turned away from the light.

When Ian returned to camp, Pippa walked out to meet him. Millie heard them stop outside her tent where she sat with her head leaning against her fists.

Ian said, "Binkie? What's he doing here?"

"He's brought some dreadful news. Harry Lewis has been killed. Let's have a drink. I was waiting for you."

"You've been crying, too," he said. "Your eyes – no, it's only the one. One of your eyes is red as anything."

"It's the same one you looked at. A filament from a grain or a seed – it flew on to the cornea and stuck there. Binkie said the tissues were about to grow over it."

They walked away, talking in low voices. Millie didn't move. Much later she heard another landrover drive towards the car park. She rolled over on her cot and put her arm across her eyes. She was lying in the same position when Stan entered the tent.

He talked about the events of the day, about Bernhard's balloon and the interview with the men in the village. She told him that Rupert Hatchard had come out from town, but Stan interrupted. The folktale was more interesting. As he spoke, he became increasingly engrossed in the subject of the lion god.

"No wedding, after all," she said.

"That's the interesting part. This is where I think it leads to human sacrifice."

"Oh no, Stan. I don't think so."

"Well, I do. And it's my field. The only trouble is, we're going to have a hell of a time trying to get in there to take a look at what's going on. Residents only."

"If it really is their religion, why would they want outsiders?"

"Why not?"

"Not if he's just died."

"Died?"

"Gone back to his people, you said."

"Oh, I see. Well –"

"They might ask you to a wedding, but not to a funeral."

"But this is supposed to be the wedding. Nicholas thinks it might be connected with ivory poachers."

"Oh?"

"You really don't feel so good?"

"I've felt a little knocked out by the sun lately."

"Come have a drink?"

"I don't think so."

He leaned over and put the heel of his hand on to her forehead.

"My father used to do that when I was a child," she said. "I can't feel anything that way. My hands are always colder than my forehead, at least I think they are. I can only find out by using the inside of my wrist. Actually, I can't even tell that way."

"Come keep me company," he said.

"All right. I'll be along in a minute."

When she sat down in the dining tent, Ian was telling Stan, "We've had some bad news. A friend of ours has died."

"Oh. That's too bad. I'm sorry." Stan looked at the rest of the company and said, "I guess it was unexpected? Not old age or sickness?"

"He was murdered," Rupert said. "Although some people are saying it was suicide."

"Impossible," Pippa and Nicholas both said.

"And other people claim his ex-wife's family had a hand in it."

Millie said, "That's nonsense. He got along very well with all of them."

"I know. You wouldn't credit what some of our self-appointed expert gossipmongers will say. One of the stories these people have hit on is that he was trying to get custody of the children."

"He could see them whenever he wanted to," Millie said. "And he had lots of other children, too. Nobody who knew him would take that seriously."

"Who is this guy?" Stan asked.

"Henry Lewis," Millie told him. "He was at that party we went to. You know, at Colonel Armstrong's house."

"How can you tell all that from only meeting him once?"

"He was one of those people you know right away," she said, "as though you've known them for years. I just fell in love with him."

"Yes," Pippa said. "I can't think of him gone."

"I'm beginning to get the feeling we went to different parties," Stan said.

"You were talking about *sub judice* for an hour and a half in the next room and getting plastered. Remember?"

"Sure. What's happened about that? The man that got pushed out of his car in the game park."

"Even more theories about that," Rupert said.

"What's the odds?" Ian asked.

"The woman will get off. And – it's curious you should say that. Thousands of people are making book on it. I think the three of them will be acquitted in the end. They're backing each other up, that's the main thing. Afterwards they can thrash out the question of who gets what. Place your bets, ladies and gentlemen."

"Yes, I suppose there's money in it, too," Pippa said. "That always makes crime interesting."

"It makes crime happen," said Nicholas. Ian took a deep breath and let it go. He ran a hand over his face. Pippa made a tentative motion towards her bad eye and stopped. They all had extra drinks; all, except Millie.

After dinner Stan said to her that he'd like to take a walk but Nicholas had warned him not to, because of the lion.

"That was weird," she told him. "He walked straight towards me, like he was going to come right up to my face and say hello."

"You must have been paralyzed."

"I was like somebody who's stuck his finger in the light socket. Thrilled and shocked. And I knew – totally, all over – that nothing I could do would stop it. If Nicholas hadn't spoken, I think I'd have started to go out of my mind. I mean it. I had this feeling that he'd come to get me. It was so strange. I can't describe it. If he hadn't intended to charge, I'd have done something to make him. I wouldn't have been able to help it."

"Panic."

"Um."

"This guy, Lewis. What was he like?"

"Wonderful. He was wonderful."

"I just realized, he's the same one Ian told me about, who got his brotherhood spearing a lion."

"Yes, he told me about that."

"You two sure covered a lot of ground in an hour and a half."

"Yes. I told you. It was like meeting someone you've known all your life."

"I know. Parties. It helps to be drunk."

Millie thought: *I should say it now, that I wasn't drunk and neither was he. We saw each other through the window that day in town, and the next morning he picked me up and asked me to his rooms and we went there, and went to bed and stayed there for the next seven hours. And at that party, too, we were in a room at the back. We were going to get married. And we're having a baby.*

"But what was he like?"

"A man of action. Bold, ardent, playful, fun, generous. No wonder they hated him."

"Who?"

"Racketeers, or whatever they are. Running a business poaching and selling ivory. But they couldn't do it out of his territory, because all his people were loyal to him."

"What people, Millie?"

"Oh, he had this job once with the game department and everybody in the area treated him as if he were an official from before Independence: they used to come to him about any disputes, and so on. He had a big reputation already because of the lions. He could call them, make them come out and lie down near him and they wouldn't hurt him. He said it was just a trick, that you did it by the voice, like that man down in Georgia your mother told us about, who could call crows."

"You'd need plenty of nerve."

"Well, he had that."

She was crying, but silently. Stan didn't notice.

"You see, I've got this theory –"

"I know, Stan. We all know."

"No, listen. If it's possible that these cults start with a real person, this guy could be it. I've just realized. And he was about to get married, too. It all fits. Tell me some more about him."

"Not now," she said. "I want to sleep."

*

She woke, crying, and put her hands over her eyes. Her body felt tightened and sore. She tried to swallow her sobbing. Stan's breathing was slow and even.

Never see him again. Never be with him. Never anything any more.

All the camp around her was still. Gradually her weeping subsided. And then, she heard a cough outside. She sat bolt upright. It had sounded exactly like Henry, that night before they left town; when he had stood under her window. The last time she had ever seen him. No animal could make a sound like that. No animal except a human being.

Maybe it was Nicholas. That was possible. Probably it was. She turned to her other side and stared into the blackness. She tried to remember. Tears moved hotly across her face, running into her nose, her mouth, her ears.

If you were here, if you could talk. Speak to me now. If we were lying side by side or with our arms circling each other, outside around inside and inside around outside. If I could die.

*

Rupert began the drive back to town early the next morning when it was still dark. Millie was at the car park to say good-bye to him and Nicholas met her on her way to the dining tent. He said, "Are you still out and about, after your fright yesterday?"

"That's right. It wasn't you coughing last night, was it?"

"No. It must have been the lion again. Short of hunting him out, I don't know what I can do about it. Pity, but we can't have a beast like that roaming about the place for long."

They strolled through the camp as the morning light grew around them. Nicholas moved his eyes to the left and back, to the right and back.

"You really think that lion could jump out on us?"

"I don't think anything. But there's always the danger. It was curious behavior."

"Maybe he's attracted by the smell of the skins."

"I could sit up tonight, try to fire a warning shot across his bows tomorrow morning."

"Your tent is so far away from everyone else's, Nicholas. It looks like the house of a hermit."

"Oh. Come see where I've put the zebra."

She went with him into the tent, which was as large as the one she and Stan had. For one person, there was plenty of room. She sat on the bed and looked over to where Nicholas pointed, at the painting, which had been ingeniously taped to a wire and the wire attached to the canvas. He stood his rifle in the corner and sat down beside her. They both stared at the picture. She cleared her throat, about to start up a conversation, but changed her mind.

She put her hand on his wrist and said, "It's very hard for you without her, isn't it?" He lowered his head until his face almost rested against her neck. He said, "I used to think. When people said they were lonely. . . ." He swallowed. She waited for him to go on. Her wristwatch started to tick loudly. He raised his head. "I used to think it was their own fault," he said.

*

Stan was ready to leave and was going to join Joshua in the car park, when the world in front of him slowed down. Everything came to a stop. He could hear, but the sound reached him from far away. He looked out into a blazon of light and tried to concentrate. He stood completely still, hoping for the confusion to pass, for his mind to remember what he had been about to do. *Come back,* he thought. *Come back.*

And then he was standing there again, on his way to the car park. And, as always, it was as though the thing had never been.

Millie came up to him as he went by their tent. *"Bon voyage,"* she said. She moved forward, as if preparing to give him a goodbye kiss. He pulled back, and said, "Don't peck at me like that. It's such an insult."

"You don't like it? Okay."

"It isn't that I don't. It just isn't enough. Look, I'm feeling totally deprived, Millie. It's bad enough waiting for you to make up your mind about what the hell you think you're doing. And what was that Pippa said at breakfast – some kind of hint about you and Nicholas?"

"Start worrying about Rupert Hatchard. That's my idea of a man I could spend my life with."

"Oh, very funny."

"I'm serious. Not the great romance or twin souls that beat

as one, but I could be very happily married with him. Never run out of things to talk about, and put up with each other's habits."

"And you've come to the end of my conversation? Or is it my irritating habits? Don't you think we could still patch up the cracks and keep going for a little while?"

"I don't know. We may have to, I guess. I just don't know."

"What enthusiasm. How long is it going to take before you do know?"

She gave him a push with the flat of her hand. "Go on," she said. "You'll be late at the office."

He laughed. He felt for a moment that things were going to be all right. And there was something about her at last that made her seem more accessible. He had an idea that she had decided, and that the decision had been to stay together.

He got into the landrover with Nicholas and Joshua. Nicholas said, "I'll drop you two there after I talk with the man in charge. Want to see if I can find a buff Tom told me about."

They drove in silence until Joshua began to sing softly. Stan blinked at the grassland and trees, the blue sky, the long horizon. Nothing was wrong with his focus now. He'd always had good eyesight. All the good things he'd always had, never given a thought to them, and now it seemed that they were running out. But if Millie stayed, it would have to be all right.

He knew he wasn't sick. Once or twice he'd thought he might have picked up parasites from the food or the water. But that couldn't be the answer. It had started in town. He remembered how his skin had reacted to the sun at first. Maybe that was all it was – an unusual kind of photosensitivity.

*

"If they come to another line."

"What is it, like a spiderweb up there?"

"It's like the wind. Lines. We can't see them, but they're there."

The balloon floated slowly ahead of them until they thought they would be able to cut over to the right and drive across its path. And just then it picked up speed and flew high into the sky, diminishing so rapidly that it might have been a plane or a rocket.

"Look at her go," Stan said. "That's amazing."

Joshua gazed upward. He didn't seem sad or defeated, but for a long time he wouldn't look away from the place where the balloon had been. He told Stan later that he only wanted to see his friends, Bernhard and Karen. The balloon itself made him seasick; he had been up in it once and his stomach had died and died.

They took an easy route home, after trying to detach a prize gazelle from its herd. They were unsuccessful at that too, but Stan didn't mind. Joshua told him a long story about a scorpion, large parts of which, he recognized with pleasure, were almost identical to folktales from Egypt and Mexico.

*

Long before Alistair's landrover pulled up, Millie could see there was someone traveling with him.

"At last," Pippa said. "Carrol."

Alistair became shy and flushed as he introduced his fiancée. She was a nice-looking, forthright girl, slightly plump, who had easy manners and evidently liked meeting people. Pippa was delighted with her. Millie, too, wondered why Eddie had become tired of such a wife.

159

They showed Carrol everything as though she were a visitor from another planet, then they sat down to lunch. Ian said it was a pity that Rupert hadn't stayed.

"He's very broken up about Henry," Millie said. "I think he just needs to be alone for a while. He only came because he wanted us to get the true story instead of a lot of those rumors going around town."

"What's this?" Alistair asked.

They went through the story once more. Alistair wanted to know all the details. "There seems to be a terrible amount of homicidal activity in the country at the moment," he said. "More than usual, I mean."

"No worse than New York," Carrol told him.

They changed the subject and talked about making films, and about art. They went to look at the paintings. Millie presented Carrol with a picture of a bird. To Alistair she gave a picture he asked for specially: of a python about to eat a goat, which he referred to as a poodle.

"I shall treasure it," he said. "The snake looks more apprehensive than the dog. I don't know that one can blame him."

As they all said goodbye, Millie saw that Alistair had a different driver. She didn't ask why. Now there was no need to know.

*

She sat in front of her paints for a long while, looking at nothing. She thought about walking under the shadows of the trees in town, first dark, then light. She went back to the moment when he put his hand on her arm. She stared down at the ground and tried not to cry. Suddenly she remembered the talk she had had over breakfast in the hotel dining room with

Mrs. Miller, and how the old woman had said that she believed all life was a single cell. He and she, the animals, the
birds and flowers she had painted – she was related to everything now, and to the future. But without him.

"I love color," he had said. "I love it. Sometimes out here
when it's really hot, it disappears. All the color just goes,
whole bands drop out of the spectrum, like in the desert. A
couple of times recently I've caught myself thinking I miss the
snow, but not often, not much. I like being here. Especially
now."

She lifted her paintbrush and thought she would make a
picture of a flower she had seen years ago.

He'd said, "It wasn't completely accidental, you know. I
had you followed everywhere. There were about twelve of
them trying to find out where you were staying, and reporting
back to me."

After a little while, Pippa came and stood by her.

"How's the eye?" Millie asked. "Still okay?"

"All well still, thank goodness. I like that. You have a marvelous memory."

"I don't think so. I make it up. I can't really remember what
the thing looked like, just what impression it made on me.
There. Like that. It's too bad Alistair couldn't stay to talk with
Nicholas. A letter isn't the same."

"No. And it would be a great pity if that marriage broke
up."

She's talking about me being in his tent, Millie thought. "I
think so too," she said. "I think Nicholas needs all the help he
can get. He needs to talk, he needs company. He needs people
who like him and don't believe he's failed at anything. He's
lonely. He needs not to be isolated. Don't you agree?"

"Well, yes," Pippa said. "If you put it like that."

Millie almost told her about Henry, about how she had planned to leave Stan and go away with him.

"Were you married out here?" she asked.

"Indeed we were. The reception lasted for three days. I still have the newspaper cutting. It said we had a 'tired' wedding cake."

They found Stan back in camp and telling Ian about driving after the balloon. Ian kept waving away Stan's fervor. He had had enough of balloons to last any man a lifetime, he said.

It was late, but still there was no sign of Nicholas. They had tea, talked about Alistair and Carrol, and moved to the dining tent, where the evening's drinks had been set out as usual. Stan almost said he hoped everything was all right, but realized in time that it would be another of those things that wasn't done. He asked Millie if she'd like to go up in the balloon.

"Very much. You think the love-nest story is true?"

"Sure."

Pippa said, "But it doesn't really sound the sort of thing a man would allow his fiancée – well, any decent man, right there in front of him."

"Well, maybe not. Who knows?"

Who knew anything? Only when it was nearly too late, you looked up and your future went flying away from you, invisible, like Joshua's lines in the air.

It was sunset and about to grow dark when they heard the trucks approaching. The men were singing. Everyone went out to the car park.

"I was beginning to worry," Pippa whispered.

"Me, too," Millie said.

The skinners were making a fuss about something. Ian looked startled as he saw the skins of two leopards being carried past.

Nicholas came forward. "I couldn't help it," he said. "They were right on top of us. And cubs with them. More babies for you, Pippa."

Ian said, "We only just got rid of the last lot."

Nicholas washed and changed while the others went to look at the leopards. The cubs were still mewing; they sounded like mice. Stan stepped back as the women leaned forward. It struck him as odd and faintly ridiculous that they should resemble mothers peering down into a crib.

*

She dreamt that she waited at the edge of camp, between daybreak and night. She had forgotten what she was waiting for – whether for the lion, or for Alistair's driver bringing news – but a sense of urgency and pain compelled her towards whatever it was. She stared into the grayness, longing, until out of it rose a movement like the swell of an ocean wave and suddenly he was there, Henry, standing a few yards from her. He must have walked all the way from town. He put his hands to his heart and opened them out to her. She stepped forward to meet him, and woke up.

Stan slept. He was still sleeping when she woke for the second time and got up. She washed, dressed, and left the tent. And once more, just as she was about to run ahead to greet Nicholas, the lion walked towards her.

"Don't move, Millie," Nicholas whispered.

She wanted to throw herself into motion, but it was as if her legs had turned to stone and then disappeared beneath her. She was trapped there. Her head and the upper part of her body began to feel farther and farther away from the ground.

The lion had seen Nicholas moving around to the side. It wrinkled its upper lip, showed its teeth, and began a kind of pawing dance, shaking its head sideways. Its tail twitched back and forth.

"Now," Nicholas breathed softly, "start walking away very slowly. To your right."

She put one foot behind her and stepped backwards. She thought she must be moving in an awkward, jerky manner. And all the time there was a strong pull the other way, like the power of a tide running between her and the lion.

Does he want to kill me? she thought. *Is that why?* She felt that soon she was going to faint, but she kept going backwards until all at once the lion did the same thing he'd done the first time: wheeled around and raced off.

Over breakfast she said, "It looked even bigger today. It was the size of a horse."

"Sure it's the same one?" Ian asked.

"Yes," Nicholas and Millie both answered.

"What were you doing up so early, anyway?" Stan said.

"I couldn't sleep," Millie told him. "I can't stand it just lying there with my eyes open, so I might as well get up."

"Anyone seen him at any other time?" Ian asked.

Nicholas shook his head. "Let's warn everyone and leave it at that. He's such a beauty, it'd be a pity to shoot him. Unless one absolutely had to."

"You know," Stan said, "this interests me. This is kind of a funny way for a lion to act, isn't it?"

"It is, rather," Ian said. "But they're all unaccountable.

There's not a species in the land that couldn't pull some strange new habit out of a hat after you've studied it for fifty years."

"Well, I just thought: anything unusual that has to do with lions in this part of the country – we're not too far away from the territory where those legends are supposed to come from. It does seem odd that a full-grown male would seek the company of a large group of people."

"If you're thinking he's some kind of trained pet, Stan, you can think again," Nicholas said. "This is positively the most savage wild beast you've ever seen. It's like looking into the inside of a volcano."

"If you decide to go on a hunt for it, I'd like to come along."

"No, Stan," Millie said. "It's dangerous."

"Everything's dangerous."

"I've got a feeling about it."

"It would be dangerous going up in the balloon."

"Hear, hear," Ian said.

"I'll let you know," Nicholas promised. "We won't track him down unless we have to."

"What does that mean? You'll wait till it jumps on somebody here in the camp?"

"More or less."

"But that could happen any time."

"He has a point, Nick," Ian said. "What do you think?"

"I'd rather not."

"No," Millie agreed. "It would be a shame."

"That's all very fine," Pippa said.

"Raving romanticism," Stan added. "How would you feel if your friend here just got tired waiting for his breakfast and ate somebody up?"

"Let's leave it for a bit," Nicholas said. "I've told Joshua and Robert and the boys in the cookhouse."

*

During the next few days, Nicholas took Stan out to look at several different villages. Stan asked questions all the time and kept taking notes. He filled up ring binders with paper; his cardboard and plastic filing portfolios grew fat.

The lion appeared twice again in the early morning, as before. At its first return, Millie said to Nicholas, "It's true. It's as though it's coming for a purpose, or as though he'd been trained."

Nicholas shook his head. He told her, "Let's not say anything this time. I've already warned everyone to be careful."

"Do you think it was his home ground and he's reclaiming it, or something like that? That would mean he's going to keep coming back, no matter what we do."

"All right. Stan's the one who's interested. We'll follow him out of camp."

"Could you scare him off, without actually shooting him?"

"I could try. I'd try that first. But if this is his patch, he won't give it up."

In the afternoon, Nicholas told Stan that they should have an early night, get a good sleep and wake in time to track the lion.

Stan said, "I've been thinking a lot about this thing. Listen. Wouldn't you say that a good method of seizing political power would be to convince everyone that you had supernatural abilities? And you could keep other people out of the area that way. You'd be the only authority. Simba means lion, doesn't it? And this man, Simba Lewis, was good with animals. This was his district – well, not too far from here. He could have trained a cub. He could even have kept the poachers out in order to run his own illegal operations alone."

"No, he wouldn't. He wasn't like that."

"What was he like? I'm sure there's a connection."

"Oh, old Harry had a terrible reputation. Half the people here think he had some kind of magic."

"Well, maybe they're right."

"Like a medicine man. I will say, he was the finest tracker and hunter I've ever seen. It was uncanny, almost as if he could speak the language of the beasts. He knew what they were thinking."

"And was he easy to work with?"

"Yes, very easy, and generous. He'd teach you things, snippets of information, tricks and tips he'd picked up, and you wouldn't even realize how much you were learning. We got on famously in that respect. In other ways, we weren't so well suited. He always liked to have lots happening. Celebrating, letting off steam. He was a bit of a showman. And his effect on women was incredible. I was jealous as hell about that."

"But you must all attract a lot of women. In a business like this, aren't you sometimes regarded as the hired sex symbol?"

"I don't know so much. Sometimes, perhaps. In any case, I don't know how to – Bobsy Whiteacre, for instance. I think I made that worse than it might have been. What was I to do with the woman?"

"Not knowing the lady, I'm not sure. But I think what you should have done was flirted like crazy and left her standing. She probably wanted the gesture, that's all. To balance out her husband's activities. Don't you think something like that was going on?"

"Who can tell? I don't know what anyone wants. Perhaps."

*

I could change, Millie thought. Betty had changed, but only because her life had forced her to. After having the baby she hadn't wanted, Betty had said, "You can put up with a lot in life. You have to. I keep going. Why not? But I haven't changed. I feel that my life is over. I don't think it's fair, but I don't have desires any more. I've given up hope. So, I don't care. All the things I have, even the children – how good they'd be if only I'd had any choice in the matter. I'd say to myself: how lucky I am. The way things are, it's made me hate my own husband. It isn't his fault, not really. Failure. I sometimes think failure is catching."

"It's cumulative," Millie had said. "Like success. Each one reinforces the whole series."

She started to write a letter to Betty and then changed her mind. There was too much to describe and explain and she wanted to say it directly. She leaned against the edge of a packing case and looked at one of her pictures of flowers, white in a green vase.

Like her sister, she could accept the unavoidable. But, it was by accepting things that they became unavoidable in the first place. Now that he was dead, she had no faith in the outcome of events. To break with Stan in order to live on her own, called for more strength than she had at the moment.

The strength had been partly his and it was leaving her fast. There was still enough for a decision, but nothing seemed worth the effort. Maybe later she could work out some kind of career using her painting, but it wouldn't take up her whole life. Even the baby wouldn't be enough to do that.

Soon she would have to tell Stan. She had already told

Nicholas, who had guessed and asked her. She had also told him that she had been thinking of leaving Stan.

"Is it different now?" he had asked.

She had answered yes before he could finish or add anything. The reasons didn't matter. In some ways now, things still weren't different and they wouldn't be, so it was better not to talk about them. She thought about Henry; all day long, and at night when she couldn't sleep, he was there. Her memory of him was part of her as naturally as the sound of the heart in her body. She couldn't believe that it referred to nothing.

"Tell me more about your friend, Simba Lewis," Stan asked Ian. "How old was he, by the way?"

"Oh, that's hard to say. Perhaps Pippa knows. Somewhere between twenty-eight and thirty-eight. Thirty-two, four, five perhaps."

"And he was a kind of colorful character from what everybody says?"

"Well, he could drink anyone under the table and he was a great one for the ladies, if those are qualifications. And one of the best men in the profession – perhaps the best I've seen. He was a grand chap, Harry."

"Why is it, do you think, that everyone has these stories about him?"

"Well, he was immediately likable and easy to get on with. Full of jokes and stories, very friendly. And yet – he was also a strange man. Terrifying. I always thought he was slightly insane."

"In what way?"

"I've seen him do things, and get other people to do things, that were impossible. He had a terrible temper, really – not human. He always had it held back, but every once in a while you felt it was there."

"Do you mean you thought he wasn't to be trusted in certain ways?"

"No, no, no. Trust him with anything. I mean that when he wanted to use it, he had an extraordinary command over other people. Mesmerizing. And he was someone whose word you wouldn't doubt. So, you began to believe things were possible, if he said they were."

"How far do you think he exercised his ability? Do you think he turned those villages of his district into a little kingdom for himself?"

"Possibly. The people who lived there thought of him that way. They might just have handed the whole bangshoot over to him as the man best able to run it."

"A poaching empire?"

"No. Definitely not."

"Everybody's so sure about that. That's what Nick says, too."

"And he's right. If you'd known Harry, you'd realize that."

In the evening, Stan told Millie, "I've got it all figured out. Ian doesn't agree with me, but I think this guy Lewis was building up a private empire here and he encouraged a kind of admiration society. What's known in politics as a 'personality cult.' He was running some kind of a racket, probably ivory, and giving back a certain amount to the villages to keep them sweet. The old Robin Hood system."

"Ivory wasn't ever his interest," she said. "He was a known specialist for lion, not elephant."

170

"He gave Rupert Hatchard nearly all the stories in that book of his about elephants, didn't he?"

"Yes, that's true. But – well, he just wouldn't do such a thing."

"Why not? Beautiful scheme."

"He wasn't like that."

"Okay, tell me. What was he like?"

"I told you already. Direct, simple. If he thought something, he did it. He didn't sit on his thoughts. Very daring. He didn't save anything. He lived a hundred per cent. And – he was very ordinary, in a way. I mean, you felt right from the beginning that you'd known him all your life, you relaxed with him. But he also – it's like what Aunt Edna used to say about special people: he gave out, he shone. Really. I'm sure there's something in it scientifically, some kind of radiation. That's why people are called stars, or you say they have star quality – you can't see it, but it sort of pours off them. When you were with him, you felt that way, too. You started to radiate, too. You felt free. Of course, I'm not sure if a man would have been impressed in quite the same way."

"Sounds pretty fancy. You seem to have thought an awful lot about him in such a short time."

"Mm. That's what he was like."

"Go on. This is the kind of thing I want."

"Is it? Oh, for your research. Well, that's all. I don't know what else you want."

"What did he look like?"

"Very romantic, but no pretty-boy. Medium height, strong, sort of chunky. His hair – going like this, back away from his face, like the busts of Beethoven. Eyes like ... eyes...." She stopped. "He was at that party, standing right next to me. Didn't you see him?"

"I can't remember. I was plastered. Everybody says what a ladies' man he was. Is it true?"

"Yes, like a magnet. So much that he never had to do anything with it or even be aware of using it."

"But he did use it. He used all that bunch of talents to make a fortune out here."

"Stan, when you write up this thesis, are you going to name names and everything?"

"That's a thought. I'd better find out about – no, that's all right. Just leave it out about the poaching. It'll be okay. But I've got to get in and get some tapes of those songs. I think they were trying to keep us away. Nick thinks so, too."

After he had put the light out, Millie turned over in her bed. She listened. He was still awake. She said, "Stan, I'm pregnant."

There was a long silence, then he said, "I thought you couldn't."

"I know. You thought I couldn't do anything."

"I thought you couldn't, because I knew it wasn't me. I went to the doctor right at the start and got checked out."

"So did I. Just a few months after we got married."

"Jesus Christ," he said.

"You know, I meant it when I told you I was going to leave you."

"But you've changed your mind."

"I don't know. If I could wave a magic wand and say we're divorced, I'd do it. Honest. But to go through the whole thing, with lawyers and settlements and moving house – it needs a good reason. More than just lack of ... lack of everything. But there isn't anybody else. There isn't – yes, okay.

As soon as they arrived in the village Nicholas singled out an old man to talk to. They discussed something for several minutes. The man twice made a gesture in the air with his arm: slow and final, like the action of a man using a scythe.

Nicholas returned to the landrover and they began to drive on. "What next?" he asked.

"I don't know," Stan said. "What was he telling you?"

"A lot of codswallop. Shop's closed today. The gods wouldn't like it, or words to that effect."

"That's great. What did he say exactly?"

"Stan, they've got some business of their own on, or having friends round, or some such –"

"What did he say?"

"He said that these were the days of preparation and they belonged to the king. We could come back another time. In a month, was what he said. Are you joining me for the shoot?"

"Look," Joshua said. He pointed. Up in the sky the lilac and blue balloon drifted ahead on a course parallel to theirs. "We can drive to where they come down."

Nicholas shook his head. "Not me. You want to?" Stan said yes; he'd like a trip in the balloon. Nicholas got out into the road and waited for the skinners, who were traveling behind them. Stan and Joshua started out on their own.

They chased the balloon for miles, choking in dust whenever they came to a sharp bend or had to reverse. Joshua waved ecstatically and shouted. He beat his hand against the door.

"They must see us signaling," Stan said.

"They see us. Sometimes they can't stop. They ride on the lines in the air. They have to follow."

"They can't turn around?"

We'll see how it goes. But I'm not doing all the stuff I used to. If you aren't satisfied, you can do everything yourself, or you get the divorce, if you like."

"Just one thing," he said. "Does this mean I'm still married to the virgin bride, or not?"

*

Millie stepped out of the tent to join Nicholas. This time Stan came with her and he brought his rifle. Nicholas saw them approaching, touched his hat, but didn't speak. The three of them waited.

It was nearing the time at which the lion normally came into camp to prowl around, when they heard the boys from the cookhouse tent begin to sing.

The chant grew louder and more insistent, until Nicholas held his hand up, gestured that he'd return soon, and walked off in the direction of the sound.

From the distance Millie and Stan heard a slight break in the song, voices talking, and the singing continuing more quietly. Then, it was broken again and disintegrated into speech, calling, and the noise of breakfast preparations.

Nicholas came back. He said, "They don't like it. They say it should be forbidden to hunt the lion in any way, that it would bring bad luck. I told them we just wanted to scare him off."

"What did they say to that?"

"They boasted that we couldn't frighten him. I think they've taken him up as a sort of mascot. Let's wait a while longer."

Millie said, "Maybe I should get out there and walk around the places where I was the last times I saw him."

"No," Stan said quickly.

"I think today is finished anyway, but let's see."

The lion didn't come. At breakfast they talked about it. Stan advanced theories as to why no lion would hang around a camp unless for some purpose.

"Are they feeding it?" he asked. "Or leaving food?"

"Don't be daft," Ian said.

"I don't think it's such a dumb idea. You said yourself, and Nicholas, that this lion may be a kind of cookhouse pet."

"I said mascot, not pet. You couldn't possibly describe him as a pet," Nicholas said. "This is a hell of a large lion. Enormous. The finest I've seen, I think."

"I wonder why he didn't show up."

Pippa turned to Ian. "Perhaps tomorrow," she said.

"All right, we'll all have a go tomorrow." Ian rose from the table to join Oliver. "And if you want a crack at the best part of today, speak now. Home again by sundown."

Pippa shook her head. Stan asked Millie, "Are you staying here, or coming with us? I've still got to do my research. Nick has to translate for me."

"I think I might come with you."

"Have you room for one more?" Pippa said. "I've seen so many good views now, it might be rather nice to see some people."

*

They drove to a village where Nicholas had expected to meet a friend, but no one was there to greet them. When they looked closer, they realized that the whole place was deserted.

They went back and sat in the landrover. Stan said, "What's the next village? We could try that instead."

"But the next village – the point about this one was that there was someone we could talk to."

Maybe somebody had died, Stan thought, but it looked worse than that.

"Where do you think they all went? It's kind of spooky." It was like the story he had read as a boy, about the village on Greenland, which had been found completely empty of people; the food had been on the tables – everything, but no people.

"Have they taken all their belongings?"

"Not all," Nicholas said. "They're coming back."

Millie suggested, "Maybe they went off to visit the neighbors."

"A whole village?" Stan said.

"Maybe it's a big party."

"It could be," Nicholas said. "If they're preparing for their celebrations. But I don't think it's really a very brilliant idea for us to sit in on that, Stan."

"We could try. What can they do to us? Would they do anything to us if Pippa's with us?"

"If they were going to do anything," Pippa said, "I don't think I'd make a difference."

They drove on. Nicholas said that they should probably have taken someone with them who knew the local rumors: Julius or Amos.

"If you'd taken anyone, it should have been Robert," Millie told him. "He comes from someplace fairly near here."

"How do you know that?" Stan asked.

"He told me."

The next village, which was small, was also empty. But at the third, they found such a throng of people that it looked as though several villages were jammed together. There was a great deal of talking, laughing, and occasional bursts of singing. The crowd parted for them as they stepped forward, and then a line of young men tried to block their way.

"What's happening?" Millie asked.

At the sound of her voice, attention was drawn to her. A sigh went up around them. The men stood back. One of them pointed.

Stan whispered, "I think they want your necklace." He said to Nicholas, "Should she hand it over as a gesture of good will?"

Millie said, "I'm certainly not handing over my necklace to anyone."

"No," Nicholas said. "Wait."

A mass of people, at first noisy and cheerful, then rapidly becoming wildly loud and excited, bunched closely around them, screeching and yelping. Stan couldn't even get to his tape recorder to start it. He had to shout at Nicholas, "Hell of a big mob. I've got a feeling they could start pushing us. What's going on?"

"We arrived just as they were about to have a bit of singing and dancing, I expect."

"They're trying to shove Millie in another direction. Grab her other hand, Nick."

The villagers began a song. It sounded to Stan like the chant the cookhouse staff and skinners had been singing, but his ear was not attuned to the melodies or syllabification of African music. He thought the rhythms were the same. A group of children had been thrust towards Millie through the swinging crush of packed bodies. They jumped up and down, singing at her. It was touching in a way, but it was also eerie. Stan was beginning to feel rushed and scared. He was sure that at any minute, soon and suddenly, the movement and power around them was going to come to a head, everything would go out of control. And being squashed together like that couldn't be good for her health, either.

The children began to push harder. They were smiling. The young men were smiling too, but they didn't try to get too near. All of them seemed riveted by the sight of Millie, and they kept staring at her necklace.

"Nick," Stan said sharply, "let's get out of here, for God's sake. I've got the creeps."

Nicholas threw back his head and let out a high, sustained scream like a battle-cry. Afterwards there was a lull in the noise around them. He began to speak quickly. Some of the young men answered.

"What's happening?" Stan asked. His own voice was shaky.

"They say they want Millie to join the party. They want her to play the bride. That thing she's wearing is like something associated with the god, something he always wears. This is all beyond me, you know. I've never heard any of this before."

"All right," Millie said, "I'll join the dance."

"No," Stan told her. "Take off the necklace and let them have it."

"Not for anything. I don't know why you're being so free with my things. I'm the one it's supposed to belong to."

"It's getting them all excited."

"Wait till they see my Chinese earrings. I think I left them in my pocket."

"Let's get out," Stan said.

All at once, the ranks of swaying children parted. They sang the four visitors on their way. As they retreated, Nicholas said, "I told them Millie needed to be alone in order to prepare herself."

"Prepare herself for what?" Pippa asked.

"Lord knows. But it's worked."

When they reached the landrover and started off back to camp, Nicholas asked Millie about her life: had she grown up in such-and-such a place, had this number of sisters, that number of aunts, and so on.

"Yes. How did you know? I never told you all that, did I?"

"They were singing it. They were telling your story. The story of the lion's bride."

"I think I'm going out of my mind," Stan said. "Millie got here after the cult was well established. How could they know all that about her, anyway?"

"In country places, everyone always knows everything about everybody," Millie said. "Even if they don't, they make it up."

Stan said, "Look, Nick, I came here to test the validity of a thesis, to find out about a religious cult on the other side of the world, and when I get there and I'm supposed to be right in the center of it, I find out they're singing ritual songs about my wife. This just can't be."

"It's curious, certainly," Nicholas said.

"Curious? It's crazy. It's totally impossible."

"Why shouldn't people sing songs about each other?" Millie said. "Is it so different from painting a picture of somebody? I did that picture of the man shooting down the balloon, and Robert thought it was like magic. Now you think this is so strange. It seems all right to me."

Stan said, "To me it seemed like they were ready to hustle

you away into some private little ceremony where you might have been chopped up into pieces and fed to the faithful, for all I know."

"That's pitching it a bit strong," Nicholas said. "Couldn't it be that the song was there before, and that they decided to put Millie's biography into it?"

"What was it about that thing you've got on? It looks like just a gold chain."

"It comes from this part of the world, or near here," Nicholas said.

"I thought you said you bought it in London, Millie."

"That's right."

"Well, I guess in London you can buy things from anywhere. But if it does come from around here, what a coincidence. That's like one in a million. Even more."

*

During the crowding, Pippa had been elbowed in her bad eye. She hadn't told anyone at the time but when they returned to camp she said she'd like to have a sandwich in her tent and a long rest flat on her back.

The others had lunch together and looked through the mail that had arrived while they were out. There was a letter to all of them from Alistair, enclosing a short note from Jill to Nicholas. Nicholas read it and said he was going to go in to see her as soon as they got a glimpse of the lion for Stan. "It's like a child's letter," he said. " 'Dear Nick, I am very well. I hope you are well.' "

There was a letter to Millie from London, to confirm the sale of her Aunt Edna's hatpin collection. She waved it at Stan.

179

Nicholas opened the last envelope addressed to him. It was from Darleen, and asked if he – in his capacity as tour operator – could give her Otis's address, because he had disappeared.

"I'll bet he has," Stan said.

After lunch, he wanted to work on his notes. Millie moved into the tea tent to take a nap and then arrange her paints. Nicholas joined her. He sat on a packing case and looked through one of the flower catalogs. He said, "I thought I recognized the necklace the first time you put it on. They made it for him at his village to thank him for something, I forget what. He always wore it; under his shirt, but it was visible where it went across at the top. I thought he'd hit a run of bad luck in town and sold it to pay off some debt or other. But then you said you'd bought it in London."

"He gave it to me," she said.

"He wouldn't have given it to just anyone."

"No. It was like a wedding ring. I could tell you more, but he's dead."

Nicholas nodded. He picked up a tube of paint, turned it around, and put it back. He began to go through all the tubes in the box.

She said, "You're upset about your letter. But it's good that she's still able to think about doing something practical like writing. It's a good sign."

"I suppose so. I sometimes feel I'd like to chuck the whole thing."

"I know. And then you're ashamed of yourself, and so on. It's going to take a long time. Those are Pippa's special paints. I'm not even supposed to get near them. I hope you didn't squeeze any of them."

"No, only toothpaste."

"Can you paint?"

"No more than what they taught us in school."

"That puts you in my league. I challenge you to a picture race." She gave him a pad of paper. "And a brush, there. These are the right paints."

"I can't think of anything."

"Anything in the world – animal, vegetable, mineral. You're free to choose."

"All right."

Millie began a picture of one of the ballets she'd gone to in London. They faced each other, so that she couldn't see what Nicholas had chosen to do. Her painting was ready while he was still at work. She got up and moved behind him and looked; he was making a picture of an African landscape with a house in the center, and people standing around it. She thought it must be his own house and his family before Jill had the breakdown. He was so taken up with the scene, especially the small figures of the people, that he didn't look up when she left or even appear to realize she had been there.

*

The sun moved westward, the camp was quiet. Stan gave up tinkering with his tape recorder, which had been broken during the pushing and shoving at the village. He put his note-books away and said to Millie, "You know, I didn't tell you about it, but all during this trip, as soon as we got to Africa, I've been thinking a lot about my parents. And about Sandy." He had actually started to think about them before Africa, in London. But it would only confuse things to say so.

"Yes?" she said.

"I kept feeling so angry against them and against everything else. I thought it was their fault that maybe my life wasn't what I wanted it to be. But it's all right now."

He tried to explain to her how he had gradually been working through all the unseen side of his life until at last some kind of pattern had stood out clearly to him and he could accept everything. The Fosters had taken the place of his parents and because of them he could think of his mother and father without resentment and forgive them for all the things he had held against them and which they had probably never even suspected. In addition to that, the presence of Nicholas was beginning to exert some kind of healing power over the spite and envy he had felt against his brother.

And, he thought, possibly even the time spent with Jack in London – that too had been necessary, and was in its turn being exorcised by the hunt for this man Lewis's true story. He should never have doubted his ability to shape his own present and future. He ought to have changed his way of living years ago.

He said, "You know, I've been thinking of giving up the academic life."

"Yes, that might be a good thing. All your working life you've studied these stories. Why?"

"It's a true picture of the world. The poetic world, not what we see around us. There isn't any place for heroes there."

"I'm sure there is, if you look. There are always going to be heroes. As long as there are challenges or dangers or injustices. But that wasn't why you went into that particular field, was it – to study heroes?"

"Are you being sarcastic?"

"Of course not. I'm just asking. You know me: I never think of the really good remark till about a week afterwards. Anyway, if I wanted to be sarcastic, it's much too late."

"Don't say that. Please. Nothing's too late."

"We'll see," she said. "I think I'm going to try to sell my paintings as a business. You know: for a living."

"You can't. That's all changed now. The baby changes everything."

"It'll be freelance, part-time."

"Even if it's part-time, you won't have time for it."

"You know, Stan, I'm still not sure if we're getting a divorce or not."

"Are you crazy? Of course not. Not now."

"Oh. The baby?"

"Of course, the baby. What do you think?"

"What I think is that the continuation of our marriage depends on whether or not we can get along together. And if we can't, it's going to be much worse with a baby than it ever was without one. Like I said."

If she ever did try to do something about a divorce, he'd find some way of getting custody of the child. He wouldn't threaten unless she became completely unreasonable. He'd wait. And she'd come to her senses. After all, she didn't really mean it; this was a whim, like any other whim of a pregnant woman. She felt powerless to resist the force of nature within herself, so she was wielding as much power as she could over him. Better not say that, either. A few years ago, he would have. He could have explained anything to her and she would just have said, "Yes, Stan."

It would be all right. She had become so different already. That was why she had been refusing him and been distant, as though she were constantly listening for something. It was just the child, that was all. Perhaps that was the cause of everything else, too – her new beauty, her ease and charm with strangers, her radiance towards the rest of the world and her ability to draw everyone to her. It was the pregnancy. Even her clumsy paintings had about them a delightfulness that spoke directly to other people; they were part of some living design.

It was important that he too should find such a design for himself. It seemed to him now that he had been searching for it, without realizing, for many years.

And now, so he believed, he had found the key at last in the history of this character Lewis, a man about whom people had fantasies. The story of Lewis would be the basis of his best work – a popular study of the mysticism of leadership, *The Life of a Hero*: how that life became set into phrases and rituals and scenes to be acted out, how people talked about it. He would outline its development up to the stage where the discussion of events in the life became religion – a chain of symbols with their own rhythm and pattern, a large and potent drama to which the smaller lives of ordinary people made constant reference.

But the truth, the real story, was that the man had been just an opportunistic exploiter of black labor and credulity, and perhaps tribal prejudices too. A con man. He hadn't been any more of a hero than Sandy.

*

They all met by the tea tent. Ian said something felt strange about the morning; he could tell that none of his men wanted to see the thing through. They were convinced that the lion was an emblematic figure and that it would never harm them if they left it alone. It was good luck. To hunt it would be a bad thing.

"Not religious, exactly," he said. "Let's say the idea they

have is one of superstitious reverence. They consider it a magical being."

Nicholas said, "Well, I don't know that one can blame them so much. He rather has that look about him."

The sky turned from black to gray, from gray to an ebbing back of the darkness and then to a true balance between light and shade. Nicholas said, "Millie, the lion always walks towards you. He may be looking for your scent, or a sight of the clothes and colors you wear, or your face, your hair, some such thing. Would you mind walking to and fro? Only just here – it won't be far away. We'll be able to protect you at every moment. You might draw him out, if he's there. It's all right, Stan. Look, you can see."

"Okay," she said. She stepped forward, although she hoped in spite of her nervousness that the lion would never be hurt and especially would never be caught. It would be better off dead than captured. This lion was entirely different from any others she had seen in zoos, and even from all the other wild ones around them on the safari. She was pretty sure that Nicholas felt the same: he'd shoot to kill if he had to, not to capture.

She began to walk out from the circle of tents, away from cover, backwards and forwards. The air was cool and sharp, the stars fading, gray-bluish light all around turning paler. It was on a morning like this, many years ago – back in her childhood – that she had been running for a train with her parents and sisters, all of them carrying luggage. They had missed the train. And after the disappointment of the moment when they knew it was gone, her father, she remembered (who had laughed), told them that there would be another train and they'd catch that one instead. There was always another train, until one day the last one came and that was your only chance. Her father hadn't told them that part.

Stan, she thought, *this is the story you want. It's always been the same story, all along. And I forgive you, what you did to me, and to us. Everybody does those things, me too – how can people help it? It's all a mess. I'm not sorry. In spite of everything, I wouldn't take back the beginning years.*

To her left, from out of the twilight, behind the shape of Nicholas's tent, she heard a cough.

She stopped. The others had heard too, but waited to see what would happen next. She took a step forward and to the left. Nicholas, with Ian close behind him, began to glide ahead in a silent, stooping walk. Stan approached from his side, but more diffidently, breaking his stride every few seconds to peer around him.

They saw Millie, like a shadow, move as though floating or swimming, and then halt. The lion gave a deep, echoing cough, for which Stan had been stretching his hearing so hard that he didn't immediately realize the sound was there.

She stayed where she was. And then, just as the sky started to brighten, they saw the lion pace heavily from around the back of the tent and pad slowly forward towards her.

Ian drew in his breath. Ajuma whispered something to himself. Pippa sat silent and worried. Stan could hardly believe what he was seeing: it was a tremendous animal, enormous and wonderfully embodying all the majesty anyone would expect a lion to have, but which the real ones seldom possessed. A lion of lions.

It moved forward. A barrier of silence enveloped its approach; not even the night had been so still. It came nearer. And just as Millie was evidently about to take one more step, a shot rang out. The lion sprang away, heading for open land. Nicholas cursed furiously at Amos, who had fired.

"I didn't know I was doing it. It was like magic. My finger closed."

"Never mind," Ian said. "We'll track him from here."

Millie came walking back. She said, "That was much too close. You almost hit him. You almost hit me."

"Accident," Amos said.

"Well, it did what it was supposed to. He's gone, now. If he comes back tomorrow, we just do it again and he'll stop. Right?"

"It's still pretty dark," Stan said, "but that looked to me like the biggest lion I've ever seen. Wouldn't you say? Wasn't that bigger than average?"

"Yes," Nicholas said. "Superlative, in every respect. But I agree with Millie. It's hardly necessary to shoot him. A beast of that calibre should be left to sire more like him."

"We're allowed to hunt lions on our license, aren't we?"

"One or two."

"Well, that's the one or two I want. Let's go."

*

Tom and Mahola brought the food and drove the skinners when it was necessary; most of them walked with the rest of the party. For some reason, although he hadn't been hit at all, the lion was moving very slowly. Twice they saw him ahead of them in the distance. He seemed to have an ability to calculate how long it would take for them to be ready to kill after spotting him. Stan had all his telescopic sights lined up the second time, but that was just the moment Julius chose to be a little tardy in handing up the rifle; he had never hesitated before, not once. Nicholas said something in a language that wasn't Swahili.

Millie thought: *He's told the gunbearers to do everything possible to prevent anyone from getting this lion. If the others catch on, or insist on carrying their own weapons, then someone can always fall over or knock up an arm and make an excuse – for instance, just that moment noticing that the lion is of a proscribed type, then being mistaken, then not being sure about that after all.*

Stan became more excited than he had ever been on a hunt. First of all, that glimpse in the dawn light when it came forward out of the indistinct grays of its background: stealthily, and all at once, recognizably, there in front of them – immense and powerful, a foreign being, which was walking easily and without caution straight towards Millie, as though it knew her.

The moment had been so extraordinary that it had seemed to hang in the air for a time, without movement. He had felt almost entranced, as if something had been revealed to him by the appearance of the creature: an animal whose picture was as familiar to his childhood as the teddy bear but now astonishingly magnified to his perceptions by the nearness, and the enormity of experience. Only after it charged away out of camp did he realize that he had also been stupefied with terror.

Now each time the lion showed itself to the hunters, he felt an electric awareness of its presence, unlike anything he had known before. And this was not like chasing other game; he sensed that the lion was in command. It was leading them to where it wanted them to go.

Once, it rested as if to sleep. They watched for nearly ten minutes to see if it would move away from the clump of dry bushes it had chosen, but nothing happened. Amos suggested creeping along the ground and taking it by surprise. But from the place he had selected, it was definitely the lion that would be doing the watching. There would be no question of surprise.

"Then we make him charge," Oliver said.

What a cowardly thing to do, Millie thought. He wasn't hurting anyone, and they were miles away from the camp now. He wasn't even a threat.

She too had been fascinated by the way the animal had seemed to lure them on, as though trained to do it. She wondered if it might be his, the one he had told her about.

Ian and Nicholas looked at each other, signed to Joshua, and started down the slope. Stan stayed with Pippa and Millie above, and saw how the lion waited. It stayed where it was until the hunters reached just that point where the background dropped low enough to become invisible behind the bushes, and then it walked away.

He turned towards Julius, who held up his hand. To shout the information might make the lion put on speed.

He watched Ian and Nicholas work their way around to where they realized what had happened. Nicholas motioned for the rest of them to join him. Julius remained, to keep watch in case the lion moved again from the place where they had seen him go, sliding behind another screening bank of bushes.

Three times the lion employed the same trick. It was now mid-afternoon and Ian was heated and profane.

Stan said, "Have you ever seen such a sneaky bastard? Ever had a lion do this kind of thing to you before?"

Nicholas shook his head. He was amused. He looked over to where Julius and Joshua stood and said, "Let's throw in the sponge."

"Yes," Millie said.

"Yes, let's," Pippa agreed. "This isn't getting us anywhere."

"Not on your life."

"He'll just go on," Nicholas said. "Leading us a merry dance. In country like this, he could keep it up indefinitely."

"I don't believe it," Stan said.

"It's repeating everything," Pippa said to Ian, "but so are we. I don't understand why we keep doing the same thing. If we fanned out to the sides and blocked the back way, then we'd have him in a circle."

"It's not worth it," Nicholas said.

"We'd make him charge, and that would end it."

"Possibly. I don't think I'd really want to be in the way of this chap when he's on the warpath. Nor should I care to be shot by someone else in the circle."

"Well, not a real circle. If you're really going on with this, it would be a waste to go back to camp when we've come all this distance and never tried to force his hand."

"She's right," Stan said. "That goddamn animal gets us where he wants us every time, and all we've been doing as far as he's concerned is just follow orders." He was in favor of going in and taking the lion. But – although he didn't say it – he wanted to do the shooting himself. After a whole day of traipsing around and being strung along, he felt that he had earned the right to the kill.

Millie saw that his eyes were shining and his jaw set. She thought he was probably going to try to work himself into a position where he could beat everyone else to the first shot.

"I'll come too," she said.

"Not in your state. You stay here."

"You might need me to make the lion come out."

"Don't be silly. We'll have him cornered. He's going to be furious. There's no telling what he'll do."

"I can just stand there."

Nicholas said, "Better not," and Pippa told her, "I'll be stopping here."

"You can stand near Ajuma," Ian said, "if you don't get in the way." He detailed Julius to go with Stan and, after one more look at the clumped island of bushes where the lion now lay hiding, they all started off, leaving Pippa behind with Oliver. Millie would be all right; she was a good length behind Ajuma.

Nicholas and Stan took the sides. They kept on going after the others pulled up and waited. Then Ian followed behind Nicholas. Joshua and Amos trailed through the center line of the semicircle.

Stan thought the approach was wonderful. He was frightened and exhilarated at the same time, realizing that there was or soon could be a possibility of panic breaking out around him, but enjoying the thought. He knew all the separate leaves of every bush his eye fell on. He had memorized each single inch.

Everything seemed all right until he stole a look back and realized that the person coming along behind him was not Julius but Millie, and that she was walking as carelessly as if she had been sauntering through a park. He wanted to shout at her, yet he didn't dare. He made a sign with his hand, for her to get down or go back. She ignored it. He couldn't leave her like that – it was too dangerous. As he went around the curve, he would come to the stretch which they hadn't been able to see from above. The lion could be anywhere; not just in the bushes, but anywhere at all in the long grass surrounding them.

He waited for her to catch up with him. She was smiling. She looked as if she were daydreaming of pleasant things. For a moment he felt his chest clamped and squeezed by fear for her and her vulnerability and the extra life he knew she held and shouldn't be bringing into a place where there was to be a killing. And then he thought: *She's coming because she wants to be near me. She's looking at me and she's smiling.*

He put his finger to his lips, motioned her down again, and kept going forward, throwing out small stones as he went. It was only a very short time afterwards that Millie, without any kind of warning, ran past him and the lion came out as though shot by a cannon from a hummock of grass where two stones had already landed.

Joshua, sighting from behind them, said afterwards that Millie had had her arms open. He was the first to bring his rifle up, but even then it was too late.

The lion was never even hit. It struck, bolted, and was gone before Stan could think of raising his rifle. He saw only the speed of the impact, a flash of the moving body, the open-jawed head, all teeth instead of a face, and a splurge of blood, with Millie twirling in front of him and then suddenly twisted down on the ground, still.

In the days that followed Millie's death, Pippa took charge of Stan's affairs. She saw to it that telegrams were sent off to Millie's family, and to his. She packed up clothes and papers and paintings.

They held the funeral not far outside camp, at a spot where Millie and Pippa had often sat in the afternoons: she had said one day how much she liked the place. Alistair came. Rupert had been on his way when his wife was taken ill and so he had to stay with her instead, but several extra men turned up with Alistair's driver and Robert was accompanied by many friends. The service included a lot of shouting and wailing, especially from a group of people brought along by Odinga. Mourners would suddenly break out, singly or together, with a sound they had decided to contribute. It reminded Stan of a revival meeting. Dr. Adler would have loved it.

Tom looked scandalized when he heard the boys from the cookhouse chanting the same song they had sung when Millie died. They had been singing it almost without a break since then. When Stan questioned Ian about it, he was told it was "just a dirge sort of thing." He asked Tom what the words were.

Tom said, "It's some old – you know, superstition. No good. This isn't the way of the future, to have these things. We are not back in the old days, believing all that rubbish. We have cars and hospitals and universities. This is like something for the old people."

"But they're all young. What are they saying?"

"The bride goes to her husband in the marriage place. They go to their house. They eat and drink, they are happy all the time. They love each other all the time. They never grow old. They are never sick. They never thirst. All the time they have each other, all the time."

Stan stared blankly at the dry ground in front of him. He asked, "Do they always sing this when somebody dies?"

"No. This is a special song, I think. I don't know it. They

admire very much ... what happened. The masaba's bravery is a thing they can't forget. That's something like what would be a hero-thing for a man to do, but for a woman – it's unknown before. She didn't even have a knife, anything, did she?"

"No," Stan said. She just stepped forward and embraced the horror; like going into a furnace, like throwing your arms around a bomb.

*

The chanting of the skinners had sunk to a vague hum, as if retreated into the air. The days seemed suddenly soundless, they burned silently before his eyes. At night he shivered with cold. The Whiteacres wrote from the coast that in two weeks, or possibly less, they would be coming back to their camp; Ian, Ajuma and Mahola were busy getting ready for their arrival. Pippa let Stan sit saying nothing, or cry when he could, or talk. And Nicholas promised, at his insistence, that they would go get the lion. They had to, Stan said. It was a matter of principle.

It would have been a matter of principle even if it had had nothing to do with Millie. But Stan didn't say that, nor that from the moment when that blurring faceful of teeth had come flying up from the ground, his life had stopped. He knew no way of going beyond that point except to get back to it and repeat it somehow. *The mechanics of revenge,* he thought: *the ceremony in which you reproduce the previous act in a slightly altered way or with a reversed outcome, and then it cancels what took place before. Good psychology, favored by many primitive peoples and recommended in folklore. My subject, my field, my specialty.*

He waited with Nicholas through the dawn, into the early morning. Twice they kept watch but there was nothing. They drank cups of tea together. Stan was glad of the company, yet grateful that Nicholas hardly spoke; he too seemed grieved and bewildered.

"You think this is useless, don't you?" Stan asked him on the second morning.

"No, of course not. It's not the way I should feel about it myself, but I can understand it."

"It's like a personal –"

"Yes, yes. It's what I'd feel if my wife had been killed by another man. But the animal kingdom is my profession, you see. These things happen naturally, without malice. Blindly. I couldn't harbor a grudge against a brute beast. In the heat of the moment, but not afterwards."

"Even you must admit, that lion led us around. It wasn't ordinary. It was uncanny."

"It was unusual. I've seen every strange thing you can think of from lion and there's always a new exception to the rule. But it's merely instinct. None of it's conscious, like a man. Some people would agree with you, I dare say. Lion experts are all a bit dotty on the subject. They'll swear there's a mind there. Harry was an expert and he thought so."

Later that day, when they looked in on the leopard cubs, they found that one had died in the night. Nicholas lifted it out of the corner where it lay on its own. The others had moved away from it. "Before Pippa sees it," he said. "She'll go mad. She never stopped complaining about the other lot, then she was beside herself when she found they were going to be sent out of the country."

Pippa had finished the packing, handed everything over to Stan, and given him the keys. He looked bleakly at the boxes and suitcases. There was a folder full of letters, which had been put in with the painting pads. It didn't include any of Henry's letters, since Millie had finally burned them, all except one piece of the last letter she had had from him. That single sheet had been found by Pippa in Millie's jacket pocket. There had been no signature. The handwriting seemed slightly familiar, but Pippa knew it didn't belong to Stan or Nicholas. On both sides it just said, "I love you," over and over again. She left it where it was, then thought that Stan would find it, and didn't know what to do. In the end, she took it out, rolled it into a cylinder and set fire to it. Of course, the note might have been years old, in spite of its look of having been written recently – a kind of good luck charm. But really it was a mystery. She forgot about it.

"Shall we go for a walk?" she suggested. "Just a short one."

Stan agreed. He took his rifle and they set out down the road, but soon branched off. Pippa realized that on the way back they would pass by the grave in its lovely surroundings. It had been one of the nicest "good views" near the camp.

Their walk was sad and quiet until it was time to turn around; then Pippa broke into talk about Millie. She praised her poise and natural diplomacy. "That was one of the reasons why the Africans all liked her so much. It wasn't just the paintings that made her famous among them. Oh, yes – she was. Robert and Odinga were always bringing their friends to come bow to her. I used to see them during our painting sessions, like royal audiences. She was always very gracious about it – respected their dignity, never laughed. She was very patient."

Stan said, "Yes, she was," and almost broke down.

"There is one thing," Pippa said. "It's unimportant, but it upsets me. The necklace she was wearing: I put the two pieces in her shoulder bag. It was one of the first things, when I was packing up her clothes. Well, it's gone. I've looked every-where."

"You think someone in camp took it?"

"It has to be. There's no other explanation. I don't like to think it of anyone, but it was a very fine piece, and gold."

"What about the earrings? Those big gold ones she called her Chinese earrings."

"Still there. They were right in with the pieces of the chain."

"Well, it doesn't matter. Maybe you could send the earrings – or give them to me. Her sister may want them."

"Yes, all right. I'll remember."

"And that painting she did for Jill – I told you about that – and the one for Dr. Hatchard's wife: all the elephants squirting water at each other."

Pippa nodded and said yes. They turned the corner, came out near a small stand of trees and were in sight of the grave. Directly on top of the plot of earth where they had buried Millie, the lion was sitting, as still and massive as a monument and looking as though it might actually have been the head-stone of the grave.

Stan rushed forward. "You bastard!" he screamed. He slung his rifle up and began to fire, reload, and fire again.

Pippa ran to him. "What is it?" she said. She put her hand on his shoulder.

He gritted his teeth and took another sighting. The lion was gone. He lifted his head.

"Did you see it?"

"No. What? What was it?"

"You didn't see a lion there? Sitting right there, looking around so satisfied?"

"No, Stan."

"It was there. It must have run off at the first shot and I was too wound-up to notice."

"Let's look."

They approached the grave. Stan bent down to inspect the mound and the earth and grasses surrounding it. He saw no sign of animal traces, nor even of digging, which he had feared so much. He had had nightmares about the hyenas and jackals digging her up. It was important that she should be happy. The idea of animals scrabbling away at the place where she rested was more loathsome to him than anything he had ever imagined, even worse than the dream he had had years ago about the tropical insects eating the eyes out of his brother's face as he lay on his back in the jungle.

There was nothing at all. The pleasantness of the landscape around them made nonsense of his hysteria, his fears, his love, his loss, his life.

Why had he ever come there? And what reason could there have been, other than the necessity of war or starvation, so urgent that it would force a man to bring his wife to a place where she was in danger of being killed? It had been such a stupid thing to do that nothing could ever explain it.

And yet, she had loved everything about the country. She had blossomed there. And it was there that she had finally come back to him.

"Stan," Pippa said, "shall I wait for you over by the trees?"

"Yes," he said. "Just a minute." If there were no prints, no hairs, no disturbed places or crushed stalks, there had been no lion.

But that didn't matter. Forget all that. What mattered was that she had loved him after all.

She saw it before I did, he thought, *and she threw herself in front of me to save me. She did love me. She wouldn't have left. It was all the unsettling new experience of having a child, that was all; like the depressions she used to go through – they were all probably caused by hormones or something like that.*

*

Pippa mentioned the incident to Ian. He spoke to Nicholas, who said, "All right, we'll start tomorrow. See if the lion's anywhere to be seen. And if he isn't, get out and beat the bushes. Give him something to do with himself. It's better than sitting about in camp." That afternoon he talked to Stan.

Stan said, "Pippa didn't see anything. And I couldn't see a sign of him either when I got up close. She probably thinks I'm bats."

"She thinks you're going without sleep and seeing objects and movements out of the corner of your eye, rather like hallucinations. It happens frequently in bereavement. When you hear of people seeing their dead relations walking, that's what's behind it. It doesn't mean you're deranged, Stan."

He managed to laugh. He said, "You should have my job. That's just the kind of thing I used to send in to the folklore journals as an introduction: 'Ghost Stories of the Southern Highlands,' and so on. She thinks I'm crazy. She also thinks you were having an affair with my wife."

"Pippa wouldn't believe that. She knows how kind Millie was to me. She helped. I could talk to her."

"Yes, I know. Okay. Tomorrow. Do you think he's still hanging around camp?"

"No, but we'll try that first."

Stan drank an extra whisky that night. He also opened the bottle he kept in the tent, but nothing had any effect. He could tell that even if he finished off the whole bottle, it wouldn't help. Everything would only feel progressively flatter until he passed out. He borrowed a pack of cigarettes from a carton the Whiteacres had left behind, although he didn't really want them, either. They tasted bad and made his mouth smell like a room fumigated against contagion. He hadn't smoked since his early twenties.

In a way, her death was easy to understand. It had come about because among all the dangers he had thought about, he had forgotten to take the wild animals into account. He had expected trouble from people – protection rackets, politics, obstructive officials. And possibly also from the climate and local fevers or infection. But what had happened was so much simpler, and he'd overlooked it. Jack hadn't suspected, or Lavalle. Yet it was obvious. Any child who had seen a few Saturday morning movies back home could have told him: Africa was full of wild animals. Of all the world's continents, it had the biggest supply of large, ferocious four-legged animals. And they spent their entire lives killing. Killing was their life.

He looked at all the cards and papers and addresses in her wallet, put them back and pulled the photographs out of the section of plastic holders.

There they were: at home, inside their living room with the Murchisons, at his parents' house. There was her mother and father and Millie herself with her sisters and schoolfriends. There he was too, many times over, at different ages.

He remembered the slightly off-angle snapshot she had taken with Pippa's camera, of him and Pippa and Ian at the dining table in one of their first camps. But several of the other pictures he didn't know: Nicholas from the waist up and smiling, and a full-length shot of a man Stan had never seen before; the background was Africa, but the man was a stranger. There were some copies of the London street scenes he himself had done all in one morning to wind up the roll, and then another picture of the stranger, this time just of his head, which might even have been a passport photo. He put the whole bunch into his own wallet and forgot about them. He went to sleep in her bed.

In the morning, he was ready to go. He packed everything he'd need, lifted the knapsack, took his extra canteen and his rifle, and went to join Nicholas.

There was a second man standing by the tea tent, whom Stan could not make out until he came closer. It was Robert, Millie's special friend. Nicholas evidently hadn't wanted to let him come with them, but Stan didn't mind. As long as they got the lion – that was the main thing, and as long as he was the one to get it.

They waited. Time passed so slowly, he couldn't imagine the morning would come, ever, nor that his life could change from the grayness out of which something was supposed to appear, although he didn't believe it would. He wanted to lie down. He wanted to go to sleep for a year at least, but he was strung up too high for sleep. Spasms of sorrow rushed over him every few minutes like nausea or approaching unconsciousness. And then, for long periods he'd seem to blank out, not thinking of anything.

Nicholas tapped him on the arm. Stan stared ahead. He saw nothing. He saw darkness. The darkness began to move.

He raised his rifle and pushed up the safety catch. *Now,* he thought, *just as soon as I get it perfect. I'll blow you right off the earth.*

The world was still formless. The outlines, the exact definitions were not there until all at once everything was there and the lion too, hurling himself off to the side and breaking away, out of camp.

The three of them followed on foot, signaling to Amos as they went past the car park.

*

It was like the afternoon Millie died; the lion would allow them a glimpse of himself, then turn and make them follow. At the end of the first day, they had been led on in a circle almost to where they had started from, but they didn't go back to camp.

"Most peculiar damn beast," Nicholas said. They took turns to watch through the night. Anything was possible with this animal.

In the morning, Robert had a fever and couldn't stand up. "Malaria," Nicholas said. "We're not too far from camp. Shall we go on? If we lose him, we can walk home."

"Let's keep going," Stan said.

They added some extra rations of water and food to their packs and sent Amos on to the camp with Robert in the landrover.

Stan was feeling as if he too might have a fever. His eyes itched and he thought the dusty air pressed all over him like the country itself, earth and sky together breathing their heat on him. The rash he'd been afflicted with weeks before had come back. He didn't care. He didn't care about anything except the lion. He kept walking.

Every once in a while tears slipped down the corners of his bloodshot eyes. He thought he heard Millie's voice a couple of times. It came to him in pieces rather than sentences or phrases. He was aware of her having spoken – perhaps, and then the sound wasn't there. He thought back to the first apartment they'd had: the one with the broken-down stove, the old icebox out in the back hall, the luscious green bank of leaves at the windows from the tree outside, which had been his real reason for choosing the place. He remembered her opening the oven door, reaching up to the cupboards, sewing his buttons on. Her image came to him looking happy, or thoughtful, or any way – all her looks, and the gesture she sometimes used – of leaning her head a little to one side; her special look for birthdays and Christmas when she was keeping a secret, like the look she'd had recently; her sweet ineptitude if she got things mixed up. He didn't understand how he could ever have lost his temper with her. But he had, all the time. All the time. And no one had ever been as nice as Millie.

He went over their lives through all the seasons of the year. One day came back to him when they had been walking side by side, he couldn't recall exactly when, but he knew where, and it had been in the fall: they were in town during the rush hour, as the offices had let out. The sun was going down into a lingering, autumnal evening, the hurrying crowd around seemed in a good mood, all – like them – young. He'd felt that everyone was going someplace exciting, but not hurrying too much, enjoying the last of the day. Most of the trees were still green, but it was fall all right, suddenly. The air was crisp and spicy and contained a trace of smoke. They were walking home across the bridge, through the long reaches of the blue, lilac, purple dusk. The streetlights started to come on. They walked arm in arm the last few blocks. To the door, up the stairs, to the next door. The kitchen smelled like flowers from the apples she was keeping there.

*

It would have been easier if he could go on walking in a straight line and let his thoughts take their own course, but the day wasn't going to be like that. He would have to work hard to achieve his vengeance.

It was as if the lion knew. It repeated its usual strategy and they pursued, not in a circle this time but going ever deeper into the territory that belonged to the cult.

Just before noon, the animal climbed in among some rocks. Nicholas said, "You know, this is senseless. If we go on like this, we'll be trailing him clear across Africa. It's impossible, Stan."

"I have a feeling he's taking us into his own neighborhood."

"He's still in there."

"I mean, in the long run. That's what he has in mind. What's he doing?"

"Let's have something to eat while we think about it."

Stan was glad of the rest. He put his hand up to his head. All day long, beginning with the fuzzy, colorless pre-dawn, he had strained for the sight of shapes that hadn't appeared. He had been looking at everything as if his eyesight itself might call things into being. At times now the world seemed to roll over, its surfaces merging, and he felt himself ready to fall away backwards into sleep.

"It depends where he goes," Nicholas said. "We could spend the night at any one of a number of villages. But, if he heads off to where we were the other day, or farther east, then I don't know. Not if they've got those celebrations on. In that case, we'll have to leg it home. I can't think why Amos hasn't come back."

"We couldn't just sleep out in the open?"

"We could. I'd rather not have to."

They did it all the time in the army, Stan thought. Even nowadays, when war was completely mechanized; if you were deep in the jungle or wandering around out in the field, you made some kind of shelter till the morning. That was another kind of hunting, too.

A picture came to him of Sunday lunch in the summers, long ago, at his mother's parents'. And from the other side of the family: his father telling him about Uncle George and Cousin Dunstan, who went to Africa to shoot lions. And they had brought back rugs and horned heads and lots of photographs. His room – in that other grandparents' house – had had zebra-skin rugs on the floor.

Nicholas said, "I think we should turn back, you know. This chap is playing cat and mouse with us. Come back in a day or two with a team of boys and chase him out of the long grass – that's the way. All right?"

"He won't be scared. He won't chase. He didn't make a sound when the stones were hitting him. I can't leave it now, anyway."

"We'll come back. I think it's best, Stan."

"We might never find him again, and then it would always be unfinished."

Nicholas sighed. He sat silent, looking out and up at the rocks. At last he said, "Some things never finish. And one can't expect them to. I remember I once traveled through a drought area with my father. People were walking along the road, looking for a place where there was water. Only one road, everything else like burnt toast, as far as the eye could see. They were walking and crawling and dying in front of us. They lay there or pulled themselves forward on hands and knees, over the ones who couldn't move. Thousands of them. I saw for the first time how quickly people can die, and in what numbers. It doesn't bear thinking about. We were in a landrover and we had water, food, we were in the pink of health. We were going to live. We moved through the whole of it and came out untouched. There was nothing we could have done. Hundreds of thousands of them. There are some things in life that are irreconcilable. Undigestible. They don't finish. You simply have to accept them and do what you can about the other things. The droughts are going to go on. The people are going to continue to die until they leave the place. There's no way of irrigating it, and no money to carry out such a project if it were possible."

"I just have this feeling that if I don't get him and see him die, I can't leave. I've got to stay here till I get him."

"But not today. You're falling asleep. And you look like Robert. Let's go." Nicholas stood up. He held out his hand to Stan, who took it and heaved himself to his feet.

He felt dizzy and his throat was sore. But he wasn't sick. *It's grief,* he thought. *It's only grief and that will go away as soon as I kill the lion.*

"Come on," Nicholas said.

They started back. Stan felt all right now that someone had taken the decision out of his hands.

It was a beautiful day, hot but dry; a wonderful atmosphere that made everything look clean, fresh and sparkling. It was like a nightmare. The rash had ceased to have any effect on him, although he could see it in red lumps on the backs of his hands. It looked bad, but unimportant ailments were often the ones that appeared most dangerous. The really serious conditions usually remained invisible until it was too late.

"You think we'll get there before nightfall?" he asked.

"Not if we have to walk all the way," Nicholas said. "I assume they'll come back for us. Perhaps something's happened."

"But we're in a different place. How would they know?"

"Stan, you're whacked, aren't you?"

"Yes, of course."

They passed through an orchard. The road ran through the middle of it. And they saw three elephant moving slowly across their path off in the distance. Then they came to a meadow of tall yellow grasses – another one of those places that looked almost as though it could be a wheatfield from the Middle West. It seemed like a nice place. Stan kept his head turned towards it. He remembered about going out to Indiana that time to give the lecture, and how he didn't take Millie along because he didn't want to. His eyes hurt. He kept them fixed on the same place and realized suddenly that he was seeing a man standing in the field and looking back at him. He stopped.

The man was of medium height, with a strong, well-proportioned build. His hair was brown, pushed back from his forehead. His eyes were looking straight into Stan's, looking straight into them. It was the same face, the same man who was in the photographs from Millie's wallet. Stan started forward to meet him.

Nicholas yelled, but Stan didn't hear. And he didn't slow down until Nicholas's hand was on his arm, pulling him back.

"Where are you going? What are you doing? Are you mad?" Nicholas shouted at him.

Stan said, "The man out there. He's the man in the pictures."

"What man?"

He turned back to the field. There was no one there. "He

was right there just a minute ago. He was standing in the middle of the field."

"You're seeing things. You're raving."

"No. His eyes – he had a very penetrating look. He's the man in the picture."

"Wait," Nicholas told him. They both fell silent, looking at the field. A light breeze ran through the grass.

"Where did you say?"

Stan pointed.

"All right. There's something there, but not a man. Look, you can see. The grass doesn't move in quite the same –"

"That's him!" Stan called out, as they both saw the grasses break into motion and part like the waves of the sea. The lion rushed out to the side. Nicholas fired off two shots quickly, but missed. The lion kept going on into the trees until they couldn't see him any longer.

"He's turned the tables on us," Nicholas said. "Come on."

"You're going for him after all?"

"Of course. He's stalking us now. Can't have a thing like that behind us all the way home in the dark. This is one for the books, Stan."

They waded out into the field, moving carefully. Stan hated this part. He had always disliked the idea of going blind through tall grass after the large animals, but now he detested it additionally, because of Millie – even though that other field had been much easier to walk through and the grass had been only a few inches above knee-level.

Every smallest sound broke on him with tremendous force. He was afraid that if the lion charged, he would have no response left; his system would simply flood itself and stall. He'd had a car like that once. All machines, every body, could fail.

But the lion ran. Stan and Nicholas both fired and sprinted after it, ready to face it if it turned on them.

It kept going, up a hill, and the next thing they heard was screaming.

Nicholas was in front and a little to the left. Stan could see that the lion had hit a man on the other side of the rise, and that there was another man, standing, who was shooting at them.

They dropped down to the ground fast. Stan aimed at the man's legs, but the stranger had started to scuttle away towards a jeep parked behind a stand of trees.

"What's happening?" he asked. "Should I let him have it?"

"If you can bring him down without killing him."

He fired again. As the man reached the trees, he fell over to the side.

"Got him. Left foot somewhere, maybe the ankle."

Nicholas said, "Get the jeep." His voice sounded as if he were out of breath. Stan started to answer and then noticed the blood.

"He hit you?"

"Get the car, man. Go on."

It was too late. As Stan had taken his attention away, the lamed man had picked himself up, hopped over to the protection of the trees, and reached the machine. They heard the engine start.

Stan ran out into the open, down the other side of the hill. The jeep was pulling straightaway from him at an angle that made it impossible to get any clear line to the driver. He put some shots into the back tires.

Nicholas joined him by the side of the second man, who lay curled up on the ground, hands clutching his belly and his face so bleared with blood that it looked as though the skin had been taken off with a knife. Nicholas stooped down on one knee. He inspected the man's clothes and hands, without touching them, then straightened up. He went back to his knapsack, pulled it over to a rock and sat down.

"Who is it?" Stan whispered. "Do you know him?"

"His name is McBride. It took me a moment or two to recognize him."

"Why was he shooting at us?"

"I'm not sure that he was. I think the lion barged into him because he was in the way and the other one, Marcus Hart, picked up his rifle to shoot. Lion kept going and Hart saw us coming, thought we were after him for whatever he was doing out here. Poaching, perhaps. That was McBride's game."

"Is he dead?"

"Not yet. As good as."

Stan turned to the body as if to try to help. Nicholas told him it was no use: the man was bleeding to death. At most, he could be spared a few more minutes, but the procedures involved might simply serve to wake him to a conscious appreciation of his pain.

Stan said, "Okay. Let's see the arm."

"I'll need help," Nicholas told him. "Bloody shame we couldn't get the jeep."

The bullet had landed as Nicholas was drawing a bead on the running lion and turning. It had entered just above the left elbow, ploughed its way up the arm and come out at the back of the shoulder. There was a lot of blood down his back and from the upper part of the arm, where the wound was open. Stan did his best to clean everything while Nicholas cursed and told him he'd make the kind of doctor Dr. Crippen was. Then Stan took a long time doing the bandaging, which wasn't easy, since the trail of the bullet went around and up over the side. "And you'd better have some of the miracle pills, just in case," he said. He shook out a few antibiotic capsules and offered his canteen. Nicholas took the medicine and drank.

All this time, Stan realized, he hadn't thought about Millie. Suddenly she came back: her head inclined, her eyes looking down, her hand on the back of a chair. But he had been unfaithful from the beginning – he had always intended to be. And Crippen was the name of the doctor who was famous for killing his wife.

"We can't take what's-his-name with us," he said. "McBride. We'll have to come back for the body tomorrow."

Nicholas laughed. "Come back by all means. You'd be lucky to find so much as a button. Everything that can walk, creep or fly will be making a meal of him soon. Very clean country, Africa. Nothing wasted. You might go through his pockets, take his watch."

Stan knelt over McBride. There was no sign of movement. He found the watch, two knives, a wallet and some sodden papers. He tried to wipe the blood off with handfuls of grass. The wallet was completely clean and stuffed with banknotes. Nicholas stood up. Stan shouldered the knapsacks.

"I can take mine," Nicholas said.

"Just carry your rifle."

"You were right about the man in the field. I thought you were seeing things."

"It wasn't this man. At least – he's hurt so bad, it's hard to tell what he looked like, but I don't think so. Wait. I've got a picture of him. Two. Millie had them in her wallet." He brought out the two photographs and held them up. "That's who it was."

"That's Harry Lewis," Nicholas said. "You must have been dreaming, after all. He's dead."

Stan put the pictures back. They made their way carefully to the road and began the long walk home to camp.

*

They moved forward in silence. Nicholas wondered if they would be able to make camp that evening. He began to doubt it. And now he had blood on him; there would be more than one predator after that. They'd come from miles off. Stan was temporarily off his head, but he could still shoot straight. It might be all right after all. Not a soul on the road – it was extraordinary. One would think the country had been evacuated. Perhaps they really were all at some enormous ceremony. Wonderful day for it.

They walked through a shady patch of tree-covered ground and he felt uplifted by the beauty of the place.

Stan said, "I've figured it out, now. He's the lion. He found out some way of doing it. He could change back and forth. They got him in town, but unless we get him when he's a lion, he's still alive."

They came out into full sunlight again and Nicholas stumbled. At last the penny had dropped and Stan knew about Millie and Harry, but couldn't come to terms with it. This was his version. In the position they were in, it was dangerous to hold such an idea. It would be a danger even if this lion hadn't been a rogue and unpredictable. There was a point where you could ruin your life yourself, though no one else would be able to do it to you. There were people who give up just at the time when they might win. They throw it away.

"Stan, I may need your help," he said.

"I don't think there's anything we can do about it. It's like Dracula. Maybe we even need a silver bullet to kill him."

"Listen to me. I want you to give me one of the photographs of Harry."

Stan took out his wallet and handed over the picture that showed just the face of the man.

"Now, listen to me. A great many peculiar things have been going on. And no one about the place. If I can't keep walking, if we have to go our separate ways, then – you may run into strangers. I don't know what's happening, but if they threaten you and you can't make them understand anything, just hold up the picture. All right? This was his district. It should do the trick."

"Do you feel bad?"

"I'm looking ahead. You never know."

Shortly afterwards they heard shots coming from far away and followed by a short series of sounds that might have been explosions.

"Doesn't sound too good," Stan said. "What do you suppose that could be?"

"We'll find out soon enough. We're walking straight into it."

"Do you think we're going to make it?"

"You ask some bloody stupid questions, Stan. I don't know, and that's the truth."

"Yes, of course. And it hurts too, doesn't it? That was the one I wasn't going to ask. Let's talk about something."

"Perhaps later. I think we ought to save our energy."

"They say soldiers in the jungle get all kinds of problems from not being allowed to talk. It's supposed to be psychologically debilitating to march in total silence, not even being able to sing. They say it makes all the work twice as hard."

"It can be even harder, having to listen."

Two hours later they found the remains of Marcus Hart in his jeep, which had been set on fire and still reeked of burning metal and rubber and flesh. It looked as if he had been trying to change a tire, had been surprised by someone, or by several people, and had then taken shelter inside.

"They have guns?" Stan asked.

"A couple of old muskets."

"This guy Lewis could have been arming his boys."

"Not here, Stan. We muddle along without revolutions. We even got through Independence without one."

"There's nothing like one or two ideals for toppling governments."

"Of course, now they have Hart's rifle. There's that."

The sun was lower. They kept walking. Stan went off into a daze, seeming to dream while he was moving. He saw disconnected parts and scenes of past times again, images of people he knew. He thought he heard voices talking to him, and singing in a chorus.

"Stan," Nicholas said.

"What?"

"This is as far as I can go." He sat down at the side of the road on a flat stone. "Leave me one of the haversacks. And you go on. Send back a car. You have enough ammunition?"

"I'll stay with you."

"If you like. But if you get a move on now, you could make camp before it's too dark to see, and come back. Remember the photograph if there's trouble. Put it in your breast pocket, where you can get at it easily."

"You take the wallet we found on McBride. It's full of money."

"We'll turn it in."

"I don't see why. Pay off your mortgage."

"Honest as the day is long. I know what that is – it's the blood money they were going to pay the men in town for killing Harry. I wouldn't touch it."

"Okay. But you take charge of it."

They divided up the contents of the packs until Stan was satisfied. Then he said, "Just in case –"

"Hurry, Stan. When the light goes, you know what it's like."

Stan said that if they never met again, what last wish did Nicholas have, because he himself had none. Nicholas said that neither did he, and hurry up. They shook hands. Stan turned twice and waved.

*

They picked Nicholas up the next morning. He had lost consciousness shortly after Stan was out of sight and had lain shivering on the stone, sometimes coming out of his coma and then being pulled back into dreams. He had woken to the realization that the light was almost gone, had risen to his feet, staggered over to a clump of trees he was still able to mark out against the night sky and, after many attempts, had managed to climb up and wedge himself and his rifle into a nook, where he had once more passed out. The dawn had roused him and brought him down to the road, to begin walking again. And so the rescue team came upon him.

They also recovered the burned-out jeep, with what was left of Hart inside it. And Amos – he was the first to set foot in camp – had turned up late in the evening the day before; he had had to walk back after the landrover broke down on his way to rejoin the others. They never saw McBride, although as Nicholas had predicted, there was a button near the place where he'd been lying. And they never found Stan.

*

He had found something himself, just as the sun was giving out its last, best light before dropping into evening and sudden night. All the shadows were long, the light soft and yellow, not yet orange, not yet red. And he saw her, standing in the middle of a field, smiling at him. He couldn't believe it. She began to walk towards him, still smiling, just as she had that other time, and he went forward to meet her, until all at once he pulled up sharply. It was as if he'd fallen asleep and been woken by his head jerking back. He was standing alone in the middle of a surrounding sea of deep grass.

The sun was traveling right on the rim of the horizon. Way off in the distance was the official balloon, drifting freely along in the lovely air, much too far away to see him down there or to wonder about the significance of a shot.

It had been a trick. They had fooled him. It wasn't Millie at all, and now he was caught. But it wasn't going to work. He'd read and heard about plenty of men who came to Africa to seek an outer reflection of their own primitive impulses, and who ended up confronting the animal world in some silly way – unprepared, romanticized – and so died. He knew all about the death wish and he knew he didn't have it. He wanted to get out of there. And he'd take life at any price, on any terms, no question about it.

The grasses encompassed him like a bowl of silence ready to echo anything that came from him. Every slight movement he made caused a distinct sound of unmistakable importance. For an instant he thought again that all his actions might be

216

obliterated by his own panic, but the fear left him as soon as he realized what he had to do. He turned around quickly and began to stride back the way he had come.

From in front of him rose a low, reverberating growl. First on one side, then on the other, then in the center: prolonged, rattling snarls like anticipatory drumrolls.

He turned again. He would walk back through the field the same way he had started. It would take him away from the road but if he could reach the higher ground, he might even spend the night up a tree. He went ahead, trying not to think about what was in back of him, whether they were following now or standing still.

As he moved forward, he heard behind him a throaty rumbling, succeeded by heavy grunts and impatient breathing into which the full voice would come for a moment and then fade back to a humming mutter. He kept walking steadily, not changing his pace, holding his rifle ready and with the safety catch off. The weapon was not too heavy, not too light; give them a sporting chance. But they never gave you one. This was nature, there was no way you could cleanse or make it pretty. He wanted to run.

The noises behind him began to keep pace with his movements. He couldn't tell if it was only one lion, or more than one. He didn't even know if it was the right one, looking any of the many ways he had seen it: a black shape in the twilight, a brown torso flying, a moving thing, dark or light as the sun struck its coat the color of sand.

He thought about his brother, the one they had loved the best because he was the one who had died and couldn't disappoint anyone. Forget all that. That was over and he wanted to live. He should have finished with that long before. It had kept him from living his life and prevented him from making another person happy. It had brought him here. All his studies and researches had in the end yielded only that much knowledge, useless since it came too late. The firearm he held to his shoulder was more important than any of it now, and even that wouldn't help. There was no way he was ever going to get out of that field.

He told himself that he never would have believed it could end like this. He wanted the choice, or if not that, at least the preparation. He'd certainly never dreamed of it this way, never. Yet it also seemed to him, now the time had come, that all his life he'd been there in that field, always, listening and watching.

At last, from only a few yards ahead of him, he heard a deep cough and knew it was the same one. He stood still. There was nothing to be afraid of any more. This was all there was ever going to be.

He waited. He saw Millie and his family, his past, the life he would never be able to get to because it lay outside the field. He looked down the rifle barrel and held his breath. The world in front of him was made of pale grasses, nothing else.